USELESS BAY

AMULET BOOKS
NEW YORK

M. J. BEAUFRAND

USELESS BAY

Library of Congress Cataloging-in-Publication Data

Names: Beaufrand, Mary Jane, author.
Title: Useless Bay / M. J. Beaufrand.
Description: New York : Amulet Books, 2016. | Summary:
On Whidbey Island, north of Seattle, the Gray family's quintuplets
join the search for a young boy gone missing and soon discover
deep family secrets and that crimes have been committed.
Identifiers: LCCN 2016007659 (print) | LCCN 2016022339 (ebook) | ISBN
9781419721380 (hardback) | ISBN 9781613121641 (ebook)
Subjects: | CYAC: Mystery and detective stories. | Quintuplets—Fiction.
| Missing children—Fiction. | Family secrets—Fiction.
| Islands—Fiction. | Brothers and sisters—Fiction.
Classification: LCC PZ7.B3805782 Us 2016 (print)
| LCC PZ7.B3805782 (ebook) | DDC [Fic]—dc23
LC record available at https://lccn.loc.gov/2016007659

ABRAMS The Art of Books
115 West 18th Street, New York, NY 10011
abramsbooks.com

For Juancho,
as always

PART ONE

one

PIXIE

Our dog learned obedience from a murdered man.
Before he was murdered, of course. I suppose it could've been after, which would explain why the training didn't take. Crystal ball, dark room, round table, woman with a turban . . . *Hal Liston, if you're with us, thump twice if you think Patience is a bad, bad dog.*

But the facts are weird enough without dragging mediums into it. As it happened, he taught her while he was still breathing.

Hal Liston was a dog whisperer to Seattle stars. He trained the pit bulls of Mariners, the Rottweilers and German shepherds of coffee magnates, and even a Great Dane owned by that retired movie star who always played Reluctant Stoner Hero of the Seventies.

Not that we knew any of this before we sent Patience to Liston Kennels. All we knew was that, on the sly, my brother Sammy had sent $1,600 to a breeder in Alabama and bought a bloodhound, sight unseen. It cleared out his college savings. He was only ten years old at the time (we all were), so you have to give him tactical points for scamming the banks on his own. The idea that he could hide the dog from Mom, who frequently said, "No pets. I have a hard enough time dealing with five children," was not so smart.

He said he ordered the dog because he had the wacky idea that he wanted to be involved in search-and-rescue, even though he couldn't ski or rock-climb or operate a helicopter. Kind of a romantic, our Sammy. Not a big thinker-througher.

When the dog arrived in a crate, deposited on our doorstep by the FedEx guy, Mom threw a hissy fit. "Tell me you got this beast from the pound," she said.

"Yes," Sammy said. "Yes, I did. I still have a savings account."

Which, of course, meant he didn't. The rest of us knew a storm was brewing, so we got the hell out of the house. My other three brothers—Dean and Lawford and Frank—and I hopped on our bikes and pedaled off toward Langley, which was four miles away.

We were halfway there when I considered the quivering ball of fur still cowering in a crate on our front porch.

I said, "What are we going to do about that stupid mutt?"

There were five of us, all born two minutes apart. Even at ten years old, our personalities were set. Dean, the oldest, was our leader. Captain on and off the basketball court. Lawford, the second oldest, was the enforcer. When Dean issued a command, Lawford was at his right shoulder, spoiling for a takedown. He practiced on us all the time. Third in the lineup was Sammy, the prankster and believer in improbable causes like overbred puppies. He was the kid you always see riding his bicycle off the roof into a pile of grass clippings. And when the schemes invariably led to bloodshed and broken bones, Frank, the fourth of us, was always there to sew him up and set him straight. Don't get me wrong—we were all graduates of Red Cross Senior Lifesaving, but Frank was the one who thought open head wounds were "neat." He got plenty of practice on Sammy.

I was the youngest. I was just *the Girl*. My only talent, as far as I knew, was keeping up with my four brothers, and on that particular day, remembering lost causes.

Nobody wanted to think about the dog. Dean and Frank and Lawford didn't even turn around. None of us wanted to be within miles of a Mom storm. When she was mad, her rage was bigger than a tsunami. All we could do was head for higher ground.

I didn't want to face her any more than my brothers did, but it didn't seem fair to abandon Patience just because she was overpriced. So I rode back, ditched my bike out of sight, and sneaked up the front yard so Mom wouldn't notice me. She had her Rat Pack music cranked up to cover the yelling. But it still didn't drown out Mom's voice. I heard "*. . . how long it took to save that money on my salary?*"

You've heard of the Rat Pack. Dean Martin, Frank Sinatra, Sammy Davis Jr. Those guys with slicked-back hair and fedoras who sang, "Ain't That a Kick in the Head." They played poker and paraded around with blond bombshells. It was the last part that got me. I didn't mind so much that Mom named my brothers after the Rat Pack, but she named me after the biggest blond bombshell of them all. Marilyn Monroe Gray.

Which was why it was easier, at six foot two, for me to live down the nickname Pixie.

Quietly as I could, I unlatched the crate and waited for the dog to crawl out. Which she did. Slowly.

And oh, that little round puppy belly. A belly that was attached to an actual dog, whose ears were so low she kept tripping over them. She shivered. She howled. She begged to be picked up. She begged to be put down. She begged for a drink of water. She begged for the granola bar in my back pocket.

I took her to the beach. She barked at tide pools. She snapped at sand fleas. And she sniffed. And she sniffed. And she sniffed.

Patience was real cute when she was twenty pounds. Even Mom couldn't resist her and didn't try (very hard) to send her back to the breeder.

But then she grew. A lot. And all the time Sammy should've spent obedience-training her? That went to mowing lawns and serving sno-cones at art fairs and removing tree stumps—anything to replace the money he'd "so carelessly thrown away."

Before we knew it, Patience was 150 pounds of puppy who was used to getting her way.

Then she got a taste for fresh game.

She started with quail. Then moved on to hare.

Then a rubber boa. And even once a coyote almost as big as she was, mangy and dripping gore by the time she was done with it.

My brothers and I dealt with these remains mostly by toeing them over the bluff at the end of our back yard. Let the scavengers in the mud flats below sort them out. Most corpses washed up there anyway, so what was the big deal?

The worst came when Patience took on the Pellegrinis' beloved Lhasa apso, Murphy.

I can't really blame her. Murphy was small and black and white, like a walking Oreo. But even factoring in that aspect, Patience freaked the hell out of me.

I've seen dogs nip and bark at each other before. But they've never really meant it. It was just a warning, a back off.

What Patience did was something completely different. I'd never seen an animal transform so quickly from calmly sunbathing to berserker frenzy.

I had to hand it to Sammy. He may have been the romantic of us, but he never forgot that Patience was still technically his dog. He was the one who got between the two of them while Mrs. Pellegrini screamed at the top of her lungs, "Get her off! Get her off!" Sammy thrust his hand right into the scrum and pried apart their jaws. It took so much effort I could see the veins standing out on his forearms. His shirt may have even ripped down the back, Hulk-style. He was a strong kid. We were all strong kids.

When it was over, Patience went back to scratching her ear with her hind leg, but Murphy was in shreds, and Sammy needed seven stitches in his right palm. It looked so gross, we couldn't wait to outdo him. We were a family of five. *Competitive* didn't begin to cover it. Especially in terms of injuries.

Murphy, the yippy dog who looked like cookie dough bites, lost an eye and a leg. She spent the rest of her long, fart-filled existence being led around in a dog-size chariot that supported was what left of her hindquarters. The contraption made her look like a short-snouted Roman gladiator.

The worst was the day after the attack, when Mr. Pellegrini presented us with an order from Island County Animal Control to put Patience down.

None of us could argue with him. The Pellegrinis were not witches. They were retirees in their late seventies living on a fixed income. When we mowed their lawn, they tipped us in hard butterscotch candies and lemonade that still had yellow dust at the bottom of the pitcher. They were decent people.

Plus Patience had done something terrible. We'd all seen it; there was no defending her.

But we love whom we love, I suppose, no matter how vicious. So I brought up the idea of doggy boot camp.

I'd read about this guy, Hal Liston, who operated a kennel out of Deception Pass at the northern tip of Whidbey Island, where the current was so fast and deep, the water was the churning bright blue of toilet bowl cleaner. I'm serious. It should be called Ty-D-Bol Pass. Nobody had dumped anything toxic in it—it was nature all on its own, water churning through a narrow gorge.

My brother Dean, our de facto captain, liked the idea. "We're very sorry, Mr. Pellegrini. Of course we'll pay Murphy's vet bill. But what if we give Patience another chance? This guy Liston has a rep for whipping dogs like her into shape. It's your call, of course. We'll do what you say."

I could see the look in Mr. Pellegrini's eye. It said he used to like us. And he wanted to like us now—he really did—but he was just too old and tired.

"All right, since that's what Jesus would want," he said as he crumpled up the order. "But if I hear of one more incident . . ." He didn't finish. He didn't have to.

There were lots of Christians in the neighborhood, and most of them owned guns.

Enter Hal Liston, a man who seemed nice enough but didn't understand that grunge had gone out with the nineties. In a way, he looked like we did—plaid shirt, Timberland work boots, wrinkled and muddy jeans. But he had this long brown stringy hair draped over his right eye, and a bulbous nose that made him look like some creature out of a fairy tale—and not a nice one, either. Someone who would eat you up like a billy goat if you didn't answer his riddle correctly.

He whisked Patience off to his compound in Deception Pass before we had a chance to say good-bye. My brothers and I had a family conference about it later in their bunk room, and we realized none of us liked the guy—least of all Sammy—who'd endured the storm of the century from Mom to keep that dog.

We couldn't explain why we didn't like Hal Liston. He had a smoker's voice, but so what? So did everybody in the Rod and Gun Club down the road.

"It was the hair," I told my brothers. "It made him look like a troll."

When the murdered man (still not yet murdered, of course) brought Patience back a month later, she had a medieval-looking pinch collar around her neck. Liston trained us all how to make "corrections." His gravelly voice freaked me out. "As long as Patience is on this leash, she should be okay. Sit, Patience." Quick yank on the leash, followed by a high-pitched yelp. Patience sat.

"What about when she's off-leash?" Sammy asked.

Liston squinted at him. "Off-leash? You want to control her off-leash? That's another solid month of boot camp. Two thousand bucks, kid." And he looked at our roof, with the rotting cedar shingles and weeds growing from the gutters, and he smiled a gruesome smile. Without waiting for a response, he got back into his truck, which was loaded with other people's over-bred dogs that couldn't be controlled.

At that moment, I was overcome by an urge to open the back of the truck and let them all out. All of them. No matter whose Lhasa apsos they took on. The urge was so strong, I couldn't stand still.

I hated the guy. Not just because of his looks, but because he was perfectly comfortable half-assing an important job. My four brothers and I had our faults, but not finishing a job you'd started? That was a sin. This Liston guy had to go down.

I charged toward the truck, determined to wrench it open. I knew there'd be a canine scrum, but if Sammy could deal with it, so could I. I even had my hand on the door handle when, with some kind of animal supersense, Liston turned around in the driver's seat and looked right at me. The windows were up, and the aggressive dogs were all barking and howling to be let out, so I couldn't hear what he said. But I could see his lips as he pointed at me and mouthed the words *Stay . . . Good girl.*

I froze. It was as if Liston's greasy hands had snapped a leash around my neck. I didn't want to obey him, but I did. With his greasy hair and his piercing eyes, he scared me into submission.

Then he drove off, kicking up a rooster tail of pollen in our circular drive.

I stood there staring at nothing for a while before I realized that Patience was leaning against me. Without knowing I was doing it, I was stroking her long velvety ears. Her eyes were half closed, as if she were on vacation right there in our front yard.

I made two vows that day. The first was that since I hadn't been able to rescue those other dogs, I would finish rescuing Patience.

The second was that I was not going to back down from any more bullies. The next time some alpha wanted to pick a fight with me, I would fight back.

• • •

A month later, Sammy came running into my room and said, "Hey, Pixie, whaddaya think this means?"

I didn't know what he meant, since he wasn't carrying anything and since, as we've seen, Sammy isn't long on planning. Or explaining. All I knew was that something had his dander up. His eyes were narrowed the way they were in math class.

I followed him to Mom's home office. Mom herself was nowhere to be seen. Sammy kept checking over his shoulder, like we were government spies about to hack international DEFCON codes—even though she was just a telecommuting code monkey for some gaming company.

Her e-mail was up on her monitor, with the message that had Sammy so perplexed. At first, it looked like spam—the message began, "Dear Customer." It was from Liston Kennels. The body of the message read, "We're all praying for Hal's safe return. In the meantime, we'll continue to serve you and the furry members of your family as best we can."

I read it four times. I could see why Sammy needed someone to help interpret it.

"'Safe return.' Do you think that means he's been in a hiking accident?" he said.

I wondered the same thing. So I pulled up the *Seattle Times* website, thinking I would have to dig for information, but I didn't. There was Liston's troll face right on the front page. He did not look like a happy man. The way he looked, if he could've thrown a pinch collar over all of us and given us a good yank, he would've. The headline read: *Dog Trainer to the Stars Missing, Presumed Dead.*

"Oh my God! Dean! Lawford! Frank! You have to see this!" Sammy yelled, grossed out but also excited.

Here was the story, the best we could tell: Hal Liston had an ex-wife. The ex-wife had a new boy-friend. The new boyfriend, for whatever reason (and I could imagine many, beginning with the grungy hair), did not like Hal Liston. The new boyfriend was in a rage when he left the apartment he shared with Hal Liston's ex-wife.

She, worried about what might happen, called the police. The police went to Liston Kennels and found an empty house, with a rug missing from the living room. The hardwood floors where the rug had been were a lighter shade than the boards around them and smelled strongly of bleach.

Nothing else.

What the police did find two days later was the new

boyfriend's car, abandoned in a parking lot that backed out onto a particularly deep and swift part of Puget Sound. With the toilet-cleaner kind of current.

The trunk of the car did not smell like bleach. It was saturated in blood.

None of us knew how to make sense of the story. We'd seen the guy only twice in our lives—once when he picked up our dog, and then when he dropped her off. Only Patience knew Hal Liston, and she wasn't talking.

Gradually, over the years, the incident morphed into a pickup line my brothers used on girls. "Did you know that our dog was trained by a murdered man?"

But I could never bring myself to think of it that way. Every time I opened my mouth to talk about it, I felt like someone had thrown a noose around my neck and pinched me speechless.

I will never forget the smile on Hal Liston's face when he told me to stay.

And he was never found. His body was still out there, somewhere in Puget Sound.

Useless Bay, where we live, on the southern half of Whidbey Island, is where the saltwater current vomits up what it doesn't want. After a high tide, the saltwater lagoon below our bluff is always littered with broken

Frisbees, pieces of a Styrofoam cooler, deflated Mylar balloons, and signboards for fishing companies that have been out of business for twenty years. And the rest, the rotten and stinking: corpses of harbor seals, corpses of halibut with two eyes on one side of their heads, corpses of sailboats that haven't been moored properly elsewhere.

I don't believe in predetermination. I don't believe in ghosts. I don't believe that certain people are "susceptible" to messages from the other side.

But every night before something disastrous has happened to me, I've dreamed of Hal Liston smiling his troll smile. Only, in my dreams, the salt water has had its way with him. His eyes are black holes from which hermit crabs crawl. His stringy hair is green kelp. There are Penn Cove mussels growing on his bones. He creeps ashore, and his fingertips look like tentacles, grabbing hold of everything they touch. He gnashes his teeth and whispers, *I'm not done training you yet,* and he's not talking about our dog. He's talking about me.

With one tentacled hand, he reaches for Patience, and then he crunches down on her with sharp barnacle teeth. He spits out her bones. And then he reaches again.

I am next.

Like that day on the driveway, I'm too afraid to run or fight back.

He grabs me with a slimy tentacle, dragging me toward his open mouth, which smells of bleach and dead things and abandoned hope.

Dean is the one who wakes me up on nights like this. Sometimes he slaps me; sometimes he dumps Clamato juice on my face. His methods aren't subtle, but they work. He looks down at me, thrashing on the bed, and says, "You're howling again. Why do you howl?"

Because something is coming, I want to say. But I never do, because that would mean admitting to fear— something my brothers and I never did.

I dreamed of Hal Liston the night before I met Henry Shepherd and his little brother, Grant.

I dreamed of Hal Liston the night before, six years later, the Shepherds came to our door and Grant wasn't with them.

two
HENRY

"The ferry slump," Meredith and I used to call it. Even though it wasn't the ferry slumping—it was my father's shoulders.

If you keep up with your financial news, you know that Dad, the bazillionaire venture capitalist, is a decent guy. My sister and brother and I will have to work for a living, and the rest of his money Dad's going to give away to make the world better.

But he has a weakness. He likes fast cars. And he likes to drive them fast, even our beige Lexus SUV—a vehicle so huge it takes up two lanes on the freeway.

And there's the thing you probably don't know about, which is that he likes to argue with law enforcement once he's been pulled over.

There are 31.2 miles between our house in Medina and the Whidbey Island ferry. I don't know how much those thirty miles have cost us in terms of speeding tickets, since Dad refuses to look at bills (he has people for that), but they're worth it, because once we paid the toll and maneuvered onto the ferry, Dad would release his grip on the wheel, roll down the window, and inhale a bouquet of salt air, fried fish, and bus exhaust. He would lean back in his leatherette chair and let his shoulders sag. To my dad, that smell was like crack.

The Friday before Grant disappeared, we pulled into the holding lanes and parked behind a rusty pickup with a vanity plate that read DCPTION. Somewhere behind us was a car that had our "travel team": Joyce, Dad's admin, because God forbid he'd get an idea and have to jot it down himself; Hannah, our cook; and Edgar, our go-to guy. Yuri, our security dude, had gone ahead of us. Dad liked them to remain as invisible as possible. When he was at the beach, he wanted the illusion of it being just the family, the sand, and the easy come and go of the waves.

Although that afternoon, I would've welcomed a distraction of any kind because when Dad pulled the key out of the ignition, his shoulders were still up around his ears. I was still in trouble.

My stepmother, Lyudmila, said, "Don't you want to roll down the window?"

"It's raining," he said, and began drumming his fingers on the dash.

Grant, who was sitting next to me in the middle row of the car, unbuckled his seat belt and leaned forward to put his head between Dad's and Lyudmila's.

"So are we going for soft-serve today, Dad?" he asked. On the Fridays with the full shoulder slump, Dad took Grant for "ice cream" at the clam joint as we waited for the cars to be loaded. I don't know what that swirly stuff was. It definitely wasn't dairy. It tasted amazing, though.

Dad shook his head. "No ice cream today, son."

"Why?"

"There's not enough time," Dad said. "See? The next ferry has already docked. It's unloading passengers now. We'll be next. We need to be ready."

This was a lie. Okay, a half lie. It was true—the last ferry had already pulled up to the dock and was vomiting cars—but that had never stopped Dad from getting ice cream when he was in a good mood, which he wasn't this afternoon.

I wanted to call him a liar to his face, but that would only make him madder, and he was plenty mad at me already.

Grant said aloud what I was thinking. "It's because of Henry's eye, isn't it? You don't feel like getting ice cream because Henry got beat up?"

"Not quite," Dad replied. He was still drumming his fingers on the dashboard. "It's because he broke another kid's clavicle. You know what a clavicle is, right, Grant?"

My half brother jerked his shirt to the side and fingered his collarbone. "It's this bone right here. You can't put a cast on it. So that makes it tough to treat."

"Good."

"I learned that in Emergency Medicine," Grant said. "Also that when you save a victim from drowning, you should roll them onto their side so they don't choke on their own vomit."

My brother went to this swanky, plaid elementary school. Every spring they held "awareness week" for kids in the fifth grade, when they taught the kids how to play the bongos and what an erection is.

I wanted to say my eye didn't hurt that much, but

it totally ached. Worse, Dad said I couldn't have any painkillers until I'd "learned my lesson." Which, supposedly, was not smacking someone in the boathouse with an oar and fracturing his clavicle.

"That's not it at all, Grant," Dad said.

Liar.

It would've been okay if my brother had stopped there, but Grant pressed on. He tugged on his chapped lower lip. "What does 'nail' mean?"

Dad wheeled around. "What?" he said. "What kind of stupid-ass question is that?"

You know how parents like to get together and say, "I don't care if kids swear—they hear worse from us at home"? Our family was like that. Only with a bigger vocabulary. Lyudmila, my stepmom, was Russian, and the Russian language has more swear words than any other language on earth. Or so I'm told. They even have one that means "woman who farts a lot," which I think is pretty cool.

Grant blinked. "I know that a nail is a thing you pound with a hammer. But Todd Wishlow used it like a *verb*."

I pulled up my hood and sank into the beige leather seat.

Todd Wishlow was the guy on my crew team with

the broken clavicle. The same one who'd given me a black eye. Dad said we were both lucky that it hadn't been worse, but I didn't feel so lucky.

I'd seen Todd twice since the fight, and each time he pointed at his ruined collarbone, which had a lot of sutures where the rod went in. "See this, Shepherd? This is gonna get me a full-ride scholarship wherever I want to go." Surgery, college—Dad was paying for it all. As long as Todd signed a nondisclosure agreement saying that he would lose everything if he painted me as a rage machine to any media outlet in the known universe.

I, on the other hand, got the three-hour rant. Dad said a lot of things I tried to tune out but couldn't. The one that pissed me off the most was, "How can you do this to me? How can you do this to *our family*?"

Now, in the luxury SUV, I sent vibes to Grant to leave it alone. The last thing I wanted was another mega-harangue.

I slumped farther in my seat and stared at the tight bun on my stepmother's neck. I often wondered what her hair would look like if it wasn't cemented into a certain shape. Even when we vacationed in the Kalahari, she kept her hair off her face and penciled in her eyebrows.

I would find out Sunday.

It would not be pretty.

Meanwhile, Grant wasn't done getting me in trouble.

"I think Todd said, 'I nailed Pixie, and she was fabulous.'"

"*Slobber, slobber, slobber*," Lyudmila said. I loved hearing her speak Russian. I thought it was a lovely language. But when she swore in Russian, she spat. I think every language should have swear words that require spitting. It adds emphasis.

She massaged her eyebrows, and thick, leaden gunk came off, which she wiped off her hand with Germ-B-Gone patented hand sanitizer. Which was followed by shea butter and Derma White lotion, to prevent those pesky liver spots.

That she was swearing meant she thought Todd Wishlow, whether or not he had nailed Pixie, should not be bragging about it in the Lakeside School boathouse.

Dad pounded the steering wheel with his head. The horn went off. In the holding lanes of ferry-bound cars, everyone looked at us, including the bomb-sniffing dogs and the fat toddlers eating soft-serve seaweed and getting half of it on their rompers.

And here it came.

Dad went bug-eyed. "Is that what happened, Henry?" he said.

Grant said, "I think Todd also said she was a real tiger in the . . ."

"Thanks, Grant. I think he gets the picture."

"Well? Is that true?" Dad said.

"Which part? The part where I *accidentally* hit Todd's clavicle with an oar? Or the part where he goaded me?"

Meredith spoke up from the third row. "Just for the record, he didn't nail her."

"Really? How would you know?"

"Because he's Todd Wishlow. He doesn't have the guts. He's just a little kid trying to be big."

"Will someone please tell me what 'nail' means?" Grant said.

Lyudmila said something in Russian that was probably, "We'll talk about it later. When your brother isn't around to bust more clavicles."

Don't get me wrong—Lyudmila was cool. But she wasn't *my* mom, didn't teach Meredith or me to speak Russian. At least she was cool enough to know that she shouldn't be explaining trash talking about Pixie in front of me—in any language.

Dad wasn't done. "We've talked about this, Henry. It's stupid to have a girlfriend in high school. You'll just get separated. And then, even if you get through college together, you'll grow apart, and then you'll be divorced at twenty-seven."

He wasn't talking about me and Pixie now—he was talking about him and Mom. Meredith's and my *real* mom.

It wasn't the first time I'd been able to excavate a nugget of a memory about what life for us was like *before*. Before Lyudmila, before Grant. Back in the days when Meredith and I had a real mother, and we all thought we were happy—Dad included.

What was strange, though, was that it was Pixie, whom I was *not* dating, who pulled it out of him. Dad could've given me this speech about Adelina, the exchange student from Brazil, or Kathy from advanced chem or Channing from Medina Coffee (and post office). But none of them merited "The Lecture."

Pixie did, yet he kept inviting her and her brothers down to our house on the beach on Useless Bay. "Let's set up the volleyball net right here," he would say, pointing to a place on the sand right in front of the house. Which was weird because he was usually very protective of his land and his privacy. He once threatened to throw a fence around the bluff behind the house to keep people from using the path along the dike, which, technically, was his.

He abandoned his fence plans when he got to know the Grays. He had a soft spot for them in general and Pixie in particular. They looked like summer, he said, with their blond hair and broad shoulders. Plus they were "good kids." They all had the combination to the house alarm, and when we'd be away for a while, they'd come through every so often to make sure no one had broken in and no pipes had burst.

But the main reason he kept inviting them down, I think, was that they were good with Grant. They treated my little brother like he was one of them, including him in their volleyball teams and showing him how to set and how to spike the ball from the outside. They also showed him things that we wouldn't know, like the difference between an osprey and a red-tailed hawk, and why none of the giant birds that fished in the lagoon liked the taste of spiny dogfish. (It's because they pee through their skin, in case you're wondering.)

Dad sometimes said that Pixie and her four brothers were part of the landscape. It was almost as though, a million years ago, when a glacier melted and left

Whidbey Island in Puget Sound, it had deposited the five mountainous Grays, too, complete with blond hair, sunglasses, and zinc on their noses.

Me? I thought that might have been true of her four brothers, but not of Pix herself. We'd known each other for six years, and I don't know when my attitude toward her changed. Probably when she started to fill out her bikini top and board shorts. A lot of people noticed her then.

I like to think it was more than that. In my mind, she was always on the beach with Grant, the two of them poking something interesting with a stick, Pix with one hand in her blond hair to keep it from getting in her eyes.

She was more than good to Grant. She was almost tender, and it wrecked my heart to watch them, but in a good way.

But I never told anyone that. Pixie Gray was just my weekend friend, the way she'd always been.

My black eye and Todd Wishlow's broken clavicle might've indicated otherwise.

"Pixie's not my girlfriend," I said, picking at my nails.

"Good," Dad said. "Let's keep it that way. For both your sakes. You're going to college soon. It does no good to have a serious girlfriend when you're still young."

I hated getting this speech again, but I didn't blame him. After all, Dad had married his college sweetheart, my mother, when they were both twenty-two years old.

And look how well *that* turned out.

"I think they're loading," I said as the car in front of us started up and began to move onto the ferry.

Dad turned back around and started the car. "And no more violent outbursts, all right? We can't afford for you to break any more bones."

Afterward, I thought a lot about what Lyudmila said next. As Dad maneuvered the car onto the ferry, Lyudmila put a hand on my father's arm and craned around at an impossible angle. She was a dancer and amazingly supple. "You will heal," she said to me. Then to my father, "Henry is good boy. You will be proud."

Those were her last words to me.

No, they weren't.

She and Grant didn't go missing until Sunday, and this was a Friday. So at some point she must've said, "Pass the salt" or "Take out the trash."

But we remember the things we choose to remember, I suppose. And I choose to remember this moment. That Friday, the day my eye was throbbing and her long arm was draped around the back of Dad's seat, her fingers curling the fine hairs at the nape of his neck. I choose to remember how, at this moment between a small hurt and a much bigger hurt that was to come, she managed to carve us out a tiny chunk of peace.

three

PIXIE

When the police finally came, it was Dean who was led away for questioning.

It was a Sunday night. The wind was blowing the Douglas firs sideways, and the eagles were air-surfing the gusts above the bluff.

In our living room, the sofas and chairs had been pushed aside and cushions placed at sharp edges on the floor. By the fireplace. Around the coffee table.

Lawford was practicing his takedowns. On *me*.

When he was done throwing me around, he expected me to Taser him. That's because he was taking a

Criminal Justice course after school at the police academy on the mainland, for kids who were interested in going into law enforcement. Next week he was going to have to resist a takedown and get Tasered for real, and he was really excited about it.

Which would be weird if you didn't know my family.

The doorbell rang.

Splat! Lawford threw me. My head smacked the area rug, and my legs purled over the sofa.

I heard Mom answer the door. "Hey, Rupe. What brings you out? I was just making chili for the boys. Can you come in for a bite?"

As soon as I got to my feet, Lawford had me in a choke hold, so I flipped him and went to see what Mr. Shepherd was doing at our house on a Sunday night. He should be gone by now. He and his family were weekenders. He owned all the land below our bluff, which included the lagoon and the bay. They let us walk around in it but made it clear it was his.

It was strange they were here. Especially since I knew Henry's dad earlier had to take a helicopter back to Medina because he'd forgotten that he had a meeting with the Kid Trying to Save Africa with Electricity. Why had he come back, just to get on the ferry?

It didn't make sense. Something was going on.

I joined Mom at the front door.

Mr. Shepherd was standing there in a thin Windbreaker. His hood was up over his bald head, which, even in this weather, he had to slather with SPF 50 because it was already covered with pre-carcinomas.

Next to him was Sheriff Lundquist, which was odd. I tried to think if we'd done anything more illegal than trespassing.

I'd done something wrong earlier, but at the time I hadn't been sure of the right thing to do. I only knew it wasn't what was requested of me. Besides, I'd fixed it, right? I'd brought him home.

"What's happened?" I said.

Mr. Shepherd said, "It's Grant, Pix. We can't find him."

Again, I didn't understand the need for the law. Grant came here all the time on Sunday afternoons in an elaborate game of hide-and-seek, and Mr. Shepherd always came here threatening to fence our property and spoil our view if we didn't hand him over right now. I didn't blame Mr. Shepherd for being frustrated. We knew Grant probably didn't want to face the school week. The kid was obviously ADD, and we guessed his grades were in the toilet. We felt sorry for him and played along, even knowing that it was an inconvenience—the Shepherds always had a ferry to catch and things to do.

But we didn't have Grant that particular Sunday night.

Mr. Shepherd was calm and businesslike in his demeanor.

Which is how I knew this Grant thing was serious.

Behind them, in our driveway, Henry's sister, Meredith, stood looking embarrassed, and Henry himself skulked beneath his hoodie. He hid the black eye he said he'd gotten when someone on his crew team *accidentally* smacked him in the face with an oar.

"You mean Grant's not with you guys?" Lawford said.

My brothers lined up next to me. After all, we played basketball on the same team. We were quick to box people out—too quick, in this case. But I didn't realize that until later.

Mr. Shepherd said, "What kind of dumb-ass question is that? If he were, we wouldn't be here."

Mom turned and glared at us. She packed a lot of expression into that glare. You have to when you're a single mother and the smallest of your five children (me) towers over you at six feet two and three-quarter inches. "Well? What are you hoodlums waiting for? Get your gear. Go find him." She smacked Frank with a kitchen towel.

"It's not as easy as that, Louise," Mr. Shepherd said. "Last time we saw Grant, he was out in the rowboat."

One of us had the foresight to turn down Sinatra singing about having the world on a string.

I felt blood sluice through my veins. Something was *definitely* wrong.

Mom stared at Mr. Shepherd. "In this wind? What a stupid thing to do."

"He probably wanted to pull up the crab traps." I examined my fingernails. They were hard and jagged, like something that attached itself to hulls and had to be scraped off with carving tools and Tabasco sauce.

"He wasn't alone," Mr. Shepherd said. "Henry here says he saw one of yours with him."

Mom whipped around and fixed us all with a glare. Not one of us dared look her in the eye. She was a foot shorter than her children but in some ways taller than the rest of us put together.

"Which one?" she growled. She looked at us, but she was talking to Mr. Shepherd. "Which one of you took a ten-year-old child in a boat with wind like this?"

"We don't know," Mr. Shepherd said. "It was dark. The only thing Henry knows for sure was that it wasn't Pixie." Mr. Shepherd nodded at me.

Next to Mr. Shepherd, Sheriff Lundquist chewed his gum ferociously.

In my defense, I was stupid, and my brothers and I didn't know any better.

It was a reflex.

Twelve years of school. That added up to twelve suspensions, forty-six detentions. But not one expulsion, and not one of us ever—and I mean ever—took the blame for the crime he or she committed. Instead, we assigned blame based on a rotation chart taped to the back of the bunk room door.

Whose turn was it to be in trouble?

I mean, what's the point of being a quintuplet if you can't skunk people into thinking you're not yourself? It was just a little harmless fun. Besides, we gave back to the community in so many ways. Cutting up and removing downed trees so Island Electric could fix snapped power lines. Applying tourniquets to victims of motorcycle accidents; sometimes even holding their hands as they died so the last face they saw would be a friendly one saying, "Good thing you're tough."

Until that weekend, we thought that we'd done it

all and seen it all and that our identity pranks were completely harmless.

Dean stepped forward. "It was me. Like Pixie said, Mr. Shepherd, Grant wanted to check his crab traps. So I took him out. The traps were empty, so I dropped him off in front of your house. He was on his way up the walk, and I rolled the rowboat to the garage. Grant was wet but fine."

"Yeah, see, that's the thing—the boat isn't in the garage," Mr. Shepherd replied. "Henry saw you take Grant out, but he didn't see you come back."

At times like this, people say, accusations hang in the air.

But nothing ever hangs in the air in Useless Bay. Everything roars and rages and whistles through open doors.

"Maybe you should come with me to headquarters . . . uh . . ." Sheriff Lundquist searched our faces. He searched his memory. He'd lived down the road from us all our lives and still couldn't tell us apart.

"Dean," Dean said.

"Dean. Right. We'll ask you some questions and get to the bottom of this. Since you're a minor, your mom will need to come, too."

"This is ridiculous," Mom said, and threw her

kitchen towel at Mr. Shepherd. "I don't know what you're accusing my child of, but you should know better. They'd never let anything happen to Grant."

"Maybe not intentionally," Mr. Shepherd said. "But these are a reckless bunch of boys, Louise."

Mom looked as though she wanted to scratch his eyeballs out.

Dean held her back. "It's okay, Mom. The sooner we figure out what happened, the sooner we get Grant back, right? Isn't that what's most important?"

She looked like she was going to hiss like our gas range, which dated from 1973. "Fine. I'll get my coat." She turned around. "I had better not hear that the rest of you have been sitting on your asses while we're out. Spread out. One of you go with Meredith."

"I will." Sammy said.

"Pix, you go with Henry. Take the dog with you." And turning off "That's Amore" from her Rat Pack greatest hits, Mom went off with Dean into the night.

At least Dean was saved the indignity of having to get into the back of the police cruiser, but he did have to make the walk of shame to the minivan so Mom could drive him to the Island County sheriff's department, where he'd be questioned like a delinquent.

I took Dean's jacket and boots out to the front porch for Henry, since he wouldn't come in. He threw his useless Windbreaker on the driveway and yanked the oilskin jacket and waders from me.

I also brought my emergency kit. We had five of them—one for each of us. They had flashlights and bandages and Swiss army knives and flares and walkie-talkies and EpiPens, even though it wasn't strictly legal for us to carry them in Washington State. Allergic people were supposed to carry their own, but Frank once had to perform a tracheotomy on a kid who didn't know he couldn't eat shellfish. "Never again," Frank vowed. "That kid lost his pulse way too fast."

I took the flashlight out of the emergency kit and flicked it on. Henry and I walked to the trailhead, Patience galumphing, leading the way.

I knew Henry was in bad shape because he was picking at the scars on his hands again. He did that only when he was really worked up about something.

"Don't worry," I said. "Grant'll turn up."

"Jesus Christ, will you give it a rest, Pix?" he said. "I saw you."

He snatched the flashlight from me and walked ahead.

I watched the back of his head until he was so far

away from me all I could see was the beam the flashlight threw in front of him, jumping over the Scotch broom.

I had no idea what was happening. Henry was one of the few people who could tell the five of us apart. Even in a storm. In the dark. At a distance. He would've looked for the ponytail.

Why was Henry lying for me?

We both knew it wasn't Dean who took Grant out in the rowboat.

It was also true that Grant had said he'd wanted to check the crab traps. But when we got there, I realized something worse was going on from the way he was acting. Grant had barely spoken and appeared to be shivering, even though it wasn't cold outside.

What had him so worked up, I still had no idea.

And neither, from the looks of things, did Henry.

four

HENRY

Useless Bay. What a stupid name. It came from the Vancouver Expedition of 1792, when the keel of Captain Vancouver's boat hit the bottom before his anchor could. No moorage? The place must be useless.

That was the same expedition that gave the island its name, when Joseph Whidbey took a smaller boat through the treacherous waters of Deception Pass to the north of the island, proving that this body of land was an island and not a peninsula. The fact that he didn't wind up as kindling in those waters is a heroic feat in itself, worthy of having an island named after you, for sure.

But the treacherous waters were far to the north. Here, at the southern end, there didn't seem to be places for treachery to hide. Useless Bay was so shallow that a lot of beach was uncovered at low tides. So on mornings, as on the day Grant disappeared, there were plenty of things to explore. And treasure to be uncovered, if you counted money in sand dollars and moon snails, as Grant did.

It also meant that on sunny days you'd think you could walk twenty miles due south on that beach, hop across the waters of Puget Sound, and tag the Space Needle. Another ridiculous thing. At some point, the depth had to fall off because there were shipping lanes between here and there. Huge freighters came past, as did Alaskan cruises, carrying passengers and salmonella.

The tide had come in by the time Pixie took my little brother out in the rowboat. I watched them from the observatory. The rain had just begun to pick up.

Seeing them together was just one more thing that pissed me off. Grant was *my* brother. If he wanted someone to take him out in the rowboat, why not come to me? True, my association with oars hadn't been so great lately, and I had called Pixie a bitch for hooking up with Todd Wishlow, to which she'd said, "Todd who?" So my overall karma was pretty much in the toilet, and I was walking around with a pounding headache, thanks to my black eye and a lot of suppressed rage.

It was also true that we didn't need to call the law on the Grays, who were a nice family, and that I didn't need to lie about Dean going out in the rowboat, not Pix. Here was my upstanding, mature reasoning for the subterfuge: my face hurt like hell, I was mad at everything and everyone. And hey, they were big kids. They could take it. Plus this gave me more alone time with Pixie to punish her both for something she did do (take Grant out in the rowboat at high tide) and didn't do (Todd Wishlow).

When Pix and I were on our own that Sunday evening and she was supposed to hand over Grant for real, she still wouldn't tell me where she was hiding him. In fact, she denied hiding him at all.

It was true, I didn't believe the family was in on it—otherwise, they would've produced him when we showed up with the law.

But Pixie was playing it tight.

"All right," I said, when we were out of earshot of the others. "Give him up."

"Grant? Believe me, I would if I had him. This is a bad night to be hiding." She kicked at the Scotch broom that lined the walk. Yellow pollen was released into the air, then blown thirty nautical miles north of us within seconds.

Above us, on the bluff, a huge branch snapped and launched itself against the Grays' picture window.

I had to yell to be heard. "Come on, Pix. I watched you row him out into the bay."

"Yeah . . . about that," Pixie said, and summoned a stillness around her. Her dog sat at her feet, awaiting her next command. "That's what scares me. He seemed upset about something. Really upset."

I waited for her to finish her thought while the wind blew her hair into her mouth.

"Upset about what?"

"No idea. Just upset."

I waited for more. Specifics. At least a GPS location.

She didn't say anything else, but she wouldn't look at me, either. She was hiding something.

"All right," I said, rubbing the bridge of my nose, forgetting that my whole face was a wall of pain from where Todd Wishlow had banged it with an oar. "I'm really not in the mood for this. He has to be with one of you. He always comes to your house. Always at five thirty. You always find a bolt hole for him. So I'm telling you again, give him up now and we won't press charges."

Every second made my face pound more. The more I rubbed my nose, the more it hurt. The deeper the hurt, the grumpier I got. But I kept rubbing. I could feel the jelly of my eye. It was making my life hell. I had the perverse idea that if I could pop it out, I'd feel a whole lot better.

"I'm trying to tell you. We don't have Grant this time, Henry."

"Seriously? Not one of you has him."

"Nope."

"Did you ask?"

"No need."

It seemed like the Grays could communicate without talking. I called it the "psychic quintuplet network," although never to their faces. I figured I'd just get a blank stare. The quints were what they were.

But they were impressive in action.

On the school basketball court, for instance. They were legendary around the state. South Whidbey High won championship after championship. People from all over packed the bleachers just to see the magic that happened when all five of them were on the floor at the same time.

It didn't happen every play, but sometimes when they were coming down the court, the ball moved so fast you couldn't see it. Whiz bang tomahawk jam . . . *and none of them called any plays.* They weren't the tallest kids on the court, but they knew where the openings were and which one of them could do what from where. Teamwork—effortless and uncanny.

"Look, Henry, I don't think you understand how bad this is. When I rowed him back, I thought he'd go straight to you. I think I disappointed him somehow. He said he'd come to the wrong person."

At least we agreed on something. But that didn't get us any closer to finding Grant. He hadn't come to me, and I hadn't worried about it at the time because whenever he went missing he was always with *them.*

Ahead of us, Pixie's smelly dog sat perfectly still, waiting for instruction. Was this new? I don't remember Patience being so attentive before. Usually she just peed on everything and harassed squirrels until Pix whistled for her.

The dog was waiting for something. Something big. So was I.

"We already looked all over for him," Pix said.

"When?"

"When he didn't show up at five thirty, trying to avoid the six o'clock ferry."

Yeah. None of us liked going back to the mainland after two days of freedom. Grant hated it most of all. To him, Useless Bay wasn't just a retreat and the Grays' house wasn't just some broken-down rambler. It was an extension of the beach—a world filled with treasures and things of wonder, as though the Grays and all the creatures of the bay were conjured from one of Lyudmila's books of Russian folktales, where poor men talked with fish and bridegrooms danced with bears.

The wind blew the hood of Pixie's raincoat down, and her golden hair swirled around her face.

In that moment, I wondered if there was something to the urban legends about the Grays. Like the one that said they had been carved from glaciers.

Or that they had been built for a purpose.

Or that they were a sign from God.

Or the spawn of Satan.

The most broadly whispered question was: Who was their father?

No one had ever seen or heard of a Mr. Gray. The most likely theory was that he was an officer stationed temporarily at the naval base at Oak Harbor, good for one night, and that he didn't even know this brood of giants existed.

At that moment, watching the weather swirl about Pix but not affecting her, I felt something different. I wondered if the Grays weren't from any father so much as they were from the land itself—a long cold beach where it seemed you could walk forever and keep walking. A handy breed to be called up in times of crises.

The question was: Would this be one of those times? Were we in a crisis now?

It was then that I began to think beyond the pain in my face and that Dad might need the sheriff for more than to harass the Gray family. He might actually have to find my little brother.

Something might have happened to Grant. Something bad. Maybe my misdirection at the Grays' house was a stupid thing to do, because maybe my brother was really in trouble.

The important thing now was to get him back, and Pix was starting to convince me that it might be harder than I thought.

"Do you hear it?" Pix said.

"What? The wind?"

She shook her head. "Listen. I mean, really listen."

She closed her eyes and turned her face to the beach.

Even her dog—the smelly, loud one—was so silent she seemed reverent. It was like being in church.

So I closed my eyes and listened, too.

The first thing I heard was my homework list, then the little ways I'd let everybody down—as well as the bigger ones. The mistakes I'd made in the past, the ones I'd make in the future, and how I could possibly avoid them.

When I was done with those voices, then came the rip and groan of the storm, and the snore of the barn owl that seemed to be demanding, "Treat! Treat!"

But Pixie seemed to be hearing something else, something deeper. She shivered in her Windbreaker, and I couldn't understand why.

"All I hear is the wind," I said.

"Oh," Pixie said, disappointed. "Right. The wind."

I felt as though I'd failed some kind of test I didn't even know I was taking.

"If Grant's really gone, we should find Yuri. He'll know what to do," I said.

Yuri's shack was at the beach end of the trail that we were on—the one that shored up and bisected the lagoon.

"Right. Yuri," Pixie said, and she seemed to shake off something that had settled around her shoulders like a mantle. If I didn't know her and her brothers better, I'd say that she was afraid.

Even though Grant went missing all the time in circumstances that sometimes seemed even worse than this, and he had his elaborate games of hide-and-seek that often involved the Grays—who, I had to admit, took pretty good care of him when he ran off—it never made me nervous. But this was the exact moment I began to worry.

I mean, *really* worry.

Grant's disappearance was a different kind of deception.

five

PIXIE

All Henry had to say was "Yuri" and Patience forgot to stay. She shot off down the trail as though she'd been fired from a cannon. *Oh boy oh boy oh boy we're going to find things!*

Yuri had done his best to continue Patience's training where that troll Hal Liston had left off. And Yuri didn't charge us, which scored him major points in the Gray family playbook. Never mind that he had a glower that made him look like he wanted to poison you with sarin gas.

And we couldn't argue with the results. In a part

of the world filled with some of the worst smells on earth, Patience could tell the difference between a dead seagull and a dead cormorant. She did *not* eat either of them, thanks to Yuri, which was nothing short of a miracle.

There was another, worse part of Yuri's dog training that I didn't want to think about now.

I was twelve years old the night we got the first call that wasn't the neighbors saying "Get your beast to stop yowling," but instead Sheriff Lundquist saying "How good a scent hound is Patience? We're missing a toddler in the woods around Deception Pass. The parents are hysterical. Can you come?"

I remember being skeptical. There were miles of trails at Deception Pass. And, thanks to our Red Cross courses, we knew the kind of dedication it took to be a search-and-rescue team. It required months of training that Patience and I didn't have. True, Yuri had tried to plug the gaps, but it wasn't systematic.

But Mom took the phone away from me and told Sheriff Lundquist we'd be right there. Then, after rousting my brothers, she turned to me and said, "That's somebody's baby who's missing. Those parents are so desperate they're probably praying. And since no Jesus is coming, you'd better get off your ass and get going."

Mom was firmly antireligious because of all the people of faith who had gathered around her with casseroles when she was a new mother of quintuplets and promised to help . . . if only she'd repent and admit she'd been a whore to get herself knocked up to begin with.

"Hypocrites, all of them," she said. "So you be good to people while you're alive, and when you're dead, you'll be compost. Now let's go help that family find their baby."

This was before we had a system and had our kits with everything we might need in an emergency; so the five of us just had flashlights, and Frank had his roadside-assistance kit.

It was raining hard when we got to the ranger station at Deception Pass. Sheriff Lundquist briefed us on what had happened. The parents, Mr. and Mrs. Goodman, and their son, Martin, had been day-trip-ping, and they had let Martin down from his backpack for a minute—just one minute, honestly—and when they turned around, he was gone.

Now the parents were inside the ranger station, hugging each other close. Mrs. Goodman was red and poofy from crying. They were drinking hot chocolate, which Mom thought should've been spiked with Jack Daniel's.

Outside, Sheriff Lundquist handed me a flare gun and a freezer bag with a cloth diaper that had been pooped in. Full of good smells.

"Now comes the test," Sheriff Lundquist said. "Let's see if this dog really is useless. When and if you find the kid, send up the flare. We'll find you."

I alternated between not optimistic (I had the world's stupidest beast) and freaked (the kid had been missing more than eight hours—what would I find?). But I knew either way I would never be the same after that night. Either the people in uniforms gathered around me watching my dog sniff poop would remember what a failure I had been and not call me again, or I would find my first body and I'd be on the hook for the next missing hiker.

I opened the freezer bag. I thrust it under Patience's nose. "Go," I said.

And she was off.

I wasn't stupid enough to let her off the leash. Who knew what kind of sniff she'd find if I did? There were just too many distractions. So I held onto her as she plowed through the undergrowth and ran up and down muddy trails, my brothers hurrying after me.

Even though I didn't know it at the time, Dean had the presence of mind to mark the trail by breaking off branches.

Finally, Patience stopped at the top of a slope that had been eroded and went straight down into the churning water. Halfway down, a toddler, too weary to flail, was caught on a branch.

"*Aroo, aroo, aroo!*" Patience bayed, and pawed at the muddy ground. I pulled her back.

"*Harosho,*" I said. Which is Russian for *good,* a term Yuri had taught me. But I had no treats for her. A major oversight. Those would have to come later.

"Martin! Martin Goodman!" Dean called down. He didn't get a coherent response, but there was a thin mewling coming from the kid. "Pix, send up the flare. He's too precarious. We're going to have to move him. Form a chain, and let's pull him up."

"Damn it," Sammy said. I'm sure he wanted to slide all the way down on his butt. "Can I at least be on the end?"

I could see Dean's thoughts churning like the water below. "Yes," he said. We definitely didn't want Sammy on anchor. Too jumpy.

So after stepping into a clearing and sending up a flare, I wrapped myself around a Douglas fir. Frank grabbed my waist, then Lawford, then Dean, then finally Sammy, who was able to unhook little Martin from the salal and hand him up to Dean, then Lawford, then Frank, then me. As soon as we were all up top, Frank laid him flat on the ground and checked him over for broken bones and hypothermia, both of which he had.

But he was alive.

Alive enough to spread the word in the papers the next day that he'd been saved by a race of giants and one very wet princess.

Princess?

Princess?

Should we have talked poop? Should we have talked about smelly dogs? I wasn't exactly sitting at home spinning straw into gold while my brothers got out and rescued him. How long was it going to take me to live that "princess" comment down?

If I could've prayed without Mom's noticing, I would've prayed for a different superpower. It was bad enough being *the Girl*. Now I was the princess, too. I didn't see how it could get any worse.

No, that's not right. Martin Goodman could've been dead. That's how it could've been worse.

• • •

After that first rescue, my brothers and I got more calls, and we got better at finding what was lost.

Sometimes it was okay. I found hikers or paddleboarders who were cold and wet and didn't know where they were, or some adrenaline junkie who'd broken a bone, required a splint, and couldn't get cell reception to ask for it. Stupid I could handle. Injured I could handle. Scared I could handle.

It was carrying the weight of things broken beyond repair that I hated. Adult or child, it didn't matter. They were always so heavy. And even though my brothers were quick to help, I somehow felt I carried that weight alone.

No matter what configuration my brothers and I took, I was the one with the scent hound—now the best in the state, according to some—so I was the one who took the lead. I was the one who handed these broken things to inconsolable families who, if they noticed me at all, would forever associate me with the senseless death of someone they loved.

If I was a princess, I was a princess of muddy, overexposed death.

All this went through my mind as Henry and I followed Patience on the path through the lagoon to Yuri's guard shack.

Beyond the guard shack was what I thought of as the "Shepherd compound." It wasn't just a McMansion—it was the main house, a guest house they called "The Breakers," a garage where they kept their car and rowboat, and a sports court.

It was a lot of space for Grant to find a place to hide, but I didn't think he was anywhere inside. Especially not after what had happened between us earlier. And I did not want to carry Grant home.

Especially not to Henry, who was a good guy, one with a cleft in his chin and sprightly eyes and curly hair I always wanted to run my fingers through—even though he may have been acting like a butthead earlier. But hey, if my face was bruised and swollen like that, I might act like a butthead, too.

At least now he seemed to understand the seriousness of the situation.

Me? I understood it hours ago, when Grant had pleaded with me to ferry him across the great waters.

As we approached the Shepherd property, I heard something on the wind. *Stay . . . Good girl . . .* and the gnashing of teeth. Even though so far he'd visited me only in my nightmares and I was now wide awake, it sounded like the troll was abroad, creeping his way up from the depths.

I really hoped Grant hadn't tried to cross the sound in the rowboat on his own. Not only because some cruise ship might smash him to smithereens in the shipping lanes but also because something might chew him up before he even got that far.

While I was listening to voices on the wind, Henry noticed that something on the Shepherd property was wrong.

"The gate wasn't up when we left a few minutes ago," he said.

It was getting dark out. Henry waved the flashlight at the gate, and sure enough, he was right.

The Shepherds had a red-and-white gate arm that separated their manicured land from the lagoon behind them. The gate arm was useless since, if you wanted to trespass, all you needed to do was climb over or under or go around. The family relied mostly on CCTV for security and, when they weren't here, some rent-a-cop to patrol the main house and outbuildings, including the garage and the Breakers, and make sure no one was squatting in one of them.

We checked on things, too, but we had other things to do, like homework and basketball practice. People as wealthy as the Shepherds needed more protection than the five of us could provide.

And we didn't really understand the gate. It may have been useless, but it was almost always down.

Not now.

Patience was sitting in front of the shack, which meant Yuri hadn't given her three tasks yet.

That was his M.O. Three jobs, then a treat.

As Henry and I got closer and opened the door, Patience let up with the "I'm such a good girl" routine, nudged the already-open door, and started sniffing inside Yuri's shack. I heard a crash, then a whuffle.

We glanced around. Yuri was nowhere to be seen. But there was an upturned bucket of Liver Snax on the floor, the contents of which Patience was eating so fast I was pretty sure we'd see it in her barf later.

Henry yanked Patience out of the shack and examined the interior.

There was a bank of twelve monitors that displayed different rooms in Henry's family compound—the main house, the garage, and the Breakers.

The monitors were all still. There was no movement in any of them.

"Where's Yuri?" I said.

"He's probably looking for my brother, too."

"Would he just leave like that? I mean, shouldn't someone at least be here to take over for him?"

There was almost always someone sitting here—even if they were just eating Doritos and watching a Seahawks game on TV.

"Weird," Henry admitted, but he wasn't really paying attention to me. He was looking at the bank of monitors. What he'd seen must have impressed him, because he got into one of his hyperattentive states, where the rest of the world fell away.

Which was good for me, because while the monitors occupied Henry, I found Yuri's dirty little secret.

And I swiped it.

Yuri usually carried a standard-issue .44, plus a Taser and a club. But stashed in his narrow uniform closet was a Kalashnikov. He had even showed it to us once or twice. The thing always freaked me out, reminding me that the Shepherds were more than rich—that they were so rich they needed protecting. The bay windows in their estate? Bulletproof glass. And Kevlar under the carpets.

That I could handle. But I hated to think of the kind of situation where Yuri might need to fire an automatic weapon. Especially here, on the bay, where the water was so shallow and people flew kites and rode horses. Not that we didn't have our share of the darker side of things, but by the time they reached our shore, the damage was already done. The ships had come un-moored and drifted, the harbor seal was half eaten, the boots belonged to suicides who had died months before, washed down from that bridge in Vancouver.

Lawford had once loaded and unloaded the mag-azine in Yuri's Kalashnikov and later pronounced it "a piece of crap." He said it was so inaccurate you could be standing two feet away from your target and not hit it.

Sammy, on the other hand, said it was "wicked sick"—so easy to fire that even a child could use it, and many around the world did.

I swiped the wicked sick weapon from Yuri's hiding place, just because I couldn't stand thinking of it there, hiding in a place that he'd shown at least five other people.

When Henry wasn't looking, I winged it into some Scotch broom.

Something was coming. I could taste it in the air, hear it on the wind. All I could think to do was hide things for later, when I needed them.

So I camouflaged the Kalashnikov in such a way that you'd know it was there only if you looked for it. It must've been a bitch to shoulder, although I had no intention of doing that unless someone threatened Grant.

I didn't know where he'd gone, but he was the son of a wealthy man. Easy prey. I imagined him chained to a radiator, force-fed Froot Loops every other day, wallowing in his own pee, forced to poop in a bucket.

Even worse, I could practically feel his weight in my arms as I carried him home and knew that, skinny as he was, he would break me.

Firing a Kalashnikov would be nothing compared with that.

When I went back to the guard shack, Henry was still staring at Yuri's monitors. I doubted he even knew I'd been gone. He was like his dad that way—put a puzzle in front of him and the rest of the world melted away.

He was studying the monitor that pointed at the garage.

I didn't see what was so exciting that it held his attention, but Henry was Henry.

"Where is everyone?" I said. "Is Lyudmila around?"

As far as I knew, Mr. Shepherd was still searching my house for Grant, which was the logical thing to do, even though Grant wasn't there. But that left several people unaccounted for. Not just the Shepherd family, but its entourage as well: Yuri; Joyce, the super-admin; Hannah, the cook (because apparently the family couldn't even boil hot dogs on their own); and Edgar, who ran errands with a "Yes, sir" and made a hell of a spirulina smoothie.

"Wait," Henry said. He pointed to the monitor displaying the garage. "Do you see that?"

I looked to the monitor where he was pointing. There was the Lexus taking up most of the space, the rowboat in the opposite corner, the walls hung with kayaks and life preservers. I didn't understand what he was seeing.

"What's happening?"

Henry didn't look away from the bank of monitors. "The CCTV has been set on a loop."

He toggled two keys on a master keyboard.

Suddenly I understood.

In one picture the wooden rowboat—the one I'd used earlier—was in its correct place on the side of the garage.

In the second, it wasn't.

Before.

After.

Before.

After.

I didn't need to look at the time stamp to know which picture the *after* was.

The boat was gone.

Oh no. Grant wouldn't. Not by himself.

Earlier, when I'd talked to him in that rowboat, with a light mist just beginning to fall around us, crabs hadn't been on his mind.

Escape had.

He'd been so scared by something, he hadn't wanted to go back—not even to Henry. That, along with the fact that the security tapes had been tampered with, made me think that Mr. Shepherd had been right to involve the law. There was something at stake here that went beyond feuds about property boundaries or one little boy who deliberately sabotaged his busy father's schedule every Sunday night.

I hadn't understood earlier when we were out in the rowboat. I just thought he wanted to do the impossible, like my brothers and I did every day.

Please don't take me back, Pix, Grant had said when we'd rowed as far as the Shepherds' orange buoy. How hard would it be to row across the Sound?

It looks easier than it actually is. At some point, the depth drops off. The closest land off-island is Point No Point. To get there, you'd have to go through the shipping lanes. And you'd have to get past the wreck.

What wreck?

Never mind. Why do you want to go anyway? You've got nothing to prove.

I want to disappear.

I should've been more sensitive to him and asked more questions about why he wanted to get away. But he seemed to want to disappear every Sunday. So, instead, I said:

Disappear? Like that? Not on my watch, dude.

I was already sprinting out of the shack and running the perimeter of the Shepherd house, over the flagstone patio that surrounded the main building, eight motion-detector lights flicking on as I went.

I vaguely heard Henry calling, "Pix? What's going on?"

There was one thing I needed to check before I pulled in Patience to start sniffing.

The buoy. The orange one that marked where the Shepherds dropped their crab traps. I couldn't see the rowboat attached to it. But what was that? A knot of rope? Something was there. It was even darker now. I had to make sure.

I dropped my kit at the end of the Shepherds' boardwalk and was already stripping off my rain gear and sweats before I got to the water's edge. I dove and cleaved the bay like a knife.

Three feet of water. That was all it was. But the water was so cold it sent a drag with each stroke. It felt as if my arms and legs were twisted up in bulb kelp.

When I reached the buoy, I stood up. The water reached my waist.

I felt underneath. There. Thick cable covered with barnacles. Something was attached. Something that wasn't floating.

I gave the rope a good tug, expecting it to come away easily.

Instead, it had no give. There was something heavy on the other end.

I felt along the cable's length to the end and found a wooden hull. An upside-down one, covered in barnacles, but still a hull. Even under water I could tell that something was wrong. The boards were uneven or sticking up, as though someone had taken an ax to it.

My fingers probed the perimeter till they hit something soft and squishy that swayed with the ripples of the water.

I jerked my hand away.

I started to shake—and not from the cold.

I knew a dead thing when I felt it.

Maybe it wasn't what I thought it was. Maybe it was a halibut or a spiny dogfish, even though I knew the truth.

Halibut don't have fingers.

By now, Henry had found the flashlight and was standing on the back patio, shining it in my eyes, his own eye a puffed-up, plummy mess.

"Pix?" he called.

I didn't want him here. I didn't want him to see what I was afraid we'd see. I tried ignoring him.

"Pixie?" he said again.

"Stay there, Henry. Call my brothers."

The only response was a splash. I should've known. Say what you like about Henry's mood this afternoon, he wasn't the type to stand back and observe when there was an emergency.

I tugged on the cable and tugged again, but it wouldn't come free.

Henry surfaced next to me with a gasp. "What have you got, Pix?"

He wasn't ready for this. He hadn't been trained. So I tried once more to send him back.

"I can handle this on my own, Henry."

He ignored me. He reached under the water and found the hull.

I'd forgotten that he was boat-savvy. He rowed crew. Even his mess of a face was a boathouse-related injury.

He felt along the cable to where it was attached to the buoy and loosened the complex knot.

The rowboat should've floated to the surface.

It did not, but I could've told him that. There had been a drag to it when I'd tried to lift it earlier.

"All right. Let's flip it, then drag it to the beach."

"Henry . . . ," I said.

I couldn't see his expression, but I knew that even if he thought he was ready for this, he wasn't. I'd met people in his situation before. Dads mostly. People who thought they were prepared for the worst, as though there were some kind of test you could take to be ready to see a loved one who's died violently or in a stupid accident.

But there were no courses for this. If someone offers you an out, *take it.* You can see your baby brother cleaned up in the funeral home later. And you'll be better for it.

"It'll be harder to flip once we've beached it," Henry said about the boat.

Had he felt the soft tissue underneath? I didn't think so. And I didn't want him to.

"Let me take care of this. If you want to do something, call my brothers. They can help."

It was so dark out, so cold. And it was about to get worse.

I don't know exactly when Henry realized that I was trying to get rid of him, but he knew now.

"I'm not leaving, Pix. Grant is mine. I should be here."

Trying to get Henry away from here was useless.

Together, the two of us flipped the boat. It was so heavy, it didn't float any nearer the surface. So we beached it.

Henry found the flashlight where I'd dumped it on a log on my mad dash to the buoy. He shone it on the interior of the boat.

There was a pale hand, reaching directly for me, attached to long fingers, some of them still sporting jewels. The arm was attached to a lithe body and an open black mouth, as though it were going to chew me up and spit out my bones.

It was the troll from my nightmares, and yet it wasn't. Even in death, no one could ever accuse this woman of looking like a troll. She had those high Slavic cheeks. Her hair was smooth and glossy, even though the only thing keeping it in place was water.

It was Henry's stepmother, Lyudmila.

The cable was wrapped around her neck three times. I undid it and, even though I took her pulse and didn't find it, I pulled her from the rowboat and into the sand so I could perform CPR to the tune of "Stayin' Alive," because that's what you're supposed to do, even though she was too far gone for disco.

"Henry?"

I kept pounding Lyudmila's chest, but slower this time. Water dribbled out of her mouth, but it didn't seem to be doing her any good. I didn't think I'd be able to bring this one back.

A rat-a-tat-tat came from the lagoon. Some idiot was duck hunting with some serious firepower.

Henry was just standing over me, not knowing what came next.

"Call my brothers," I repeated. "We need help."

He ran up the boardwalk to where he he'd dropped his jacket on a log. I heard him rustle around and then saw his face lit up from his cell phone screen.

As soon as he was gone, something strange happened.

Water gushed out of Lyudmila's mouth, so I rolled

her to one side, even though I knew this wasn't a fairy tale. Here, in the real world, yurp up the poisoned apple and you're still dead.

I took my hands off her.

In one jerky motion, Lyudmila sat up.

I scuttled backward on the cold sand.

There could be no doubt about it: Lyudmila was gone. There was no pulse. So why was she moving? Pointing at me with a long bony finger? Staring at me with cloudy eyes?

She spoke with a voice that wasn't her own.

Stay . . . , rasped the thing that had been haunting me for years. *Good girl.*

Then I blinked, and she was a corpse again, lying on her side on the cold sand.

It took me a while to realize that I was no longer a stupid kid, the one Hal Liston had terrified motionless.

I had to remind myself I was seventeen years old now and had seen and fixed much worse.

In every emergency, I knew how to act. Why should this be any different because it was someone I knew?

I couldn't resuscitate this one, but I owed it to Henry—and to myself—to learn anything that was to be learned from what was left of his stepmother.

So I crawled closer on my hands and feet.

I closed my eyes because I didn't trust them. Instead, I listened to the howling of the wind, tasted the salt and rot on my tongue.

And I smelled.

The closer I got to her neck, the stronger the smell became. It was so strong it almost singed my nostrils off.

Someone had doused Henry's stepmother in bleach.

six

HENRY

My phone was in my jacket, which I'd left on a log, sodden with rain. Dead. Had to be. I scrubbed the phone's face with my dripping arm. I tapped every part of the screen. I got static first. Then random icons popped up and blinked out.

I couldn't think straight. My fingers were shaking too hard to push buttons. I needed Dad. He'd know what to do. How the hell was I supposed to get in touch with him now? He didn't give his phone number to just anyone. You had to earn it. Even when I called him, I always got his assistant, Joyce, first, and she decided if I was important enough to be passed on to Dad on high.

I put my head in my hands and let myself be pelted by rain. *Where the hell was Grant?*

I was going to murder the little twerp myself when he showed up.

When I looked up, Lawford and Frank had materialized, and they looked somber. At least, I *assumed* it was Lawford and Frank. I was a little stressed and their faces blurred in the rain. Lawford had his Taser out and Frank was rubber-gloved and carrying a first aid kit.

"Where's Sammy?" I said. Even after all this time, understanding their quirks and knowing their scars, I still sometimes had to guess at who was who.

"Dunno," Lawford said. "Probably still out searching with Meredith. They went off together hours ago. I don't think anyone's heard from them."

They waited for the next morsel of information.

"Tell me you've got my brother."

"Grant? Not yet. We'd hoped you and Pix had scared him up." Frank was the one who spoke first.

I shook my head. "It wasn't him we found." I pointed to where Lyudmila lay under dark skies, the tide ebbing beyond her. I couldn't see her, but I knew her face was blanched and crusted with sand. Her eyes were open. She didn't even blink them against the rain.

Pix had given up working on her and was now swimming the bay, looking for "loose ends," as she called them, which I think meant the corpse of my little brother, which might have drifted away. She thought the killing might have been some kind of two-for-one special.

But I didn't want to think about that. I was too cold to think. I'd put my shirt back on once I'd gotten out of the water, but it did little to warm me since it was wet from the rain, too.

I wasn't sure I wanted to warm up.

Meanwhile, Frank had trotted over to where we'd left Lyudmila on the beach. He put two fingers to her neck, then closed her eyes with his hands the size of hulls. He shucked off his yellow oilskin raincoat and draped it over her.

Most people would've thought this a kindness, but not me. I was pissed. He didn't even *try* to resuscitate her. I mean, he was Frank Gray. I once saw him try to give CPR to a field mouse that was so dead it'd been partially digested by a barn owl.

"That's it? You're not even going to try?" I now had three Grays. I expected miracles. Where was my goddamn miracle?

Frank said, "I'm sorry, Henry. She seemed like a really nice lady."

"Where did you find her?" Lawford said.

"In the boat. By the buoy. It had been sunk. They were really catching crabs."

I guess I'd said that last part aloud. Lawford blinked. "Pardon?"

"It's a rowing term. You know, when you scoop or get out of sequence with the guy in the stroke position? And we found the boat by where the crab traps usually are? Get it?"

Frank took a penlight out of his first-aid kit and inspected my good eye, then he pried the bad one open and looked at it, too.

That hurt.

It may have been dark out, but I saw Frank mouth the word *shock* to Lawford.

"We think you should sit down over here, out of the rain. The smart thing now is to get Pix and the dog and start looking for your brother on land."

Those were the first sensible words I'd heard in hours. When Pixie said she was going to swim the bay a little longer, it hadn't seemed very smart to me. As I said, I was too numb to think. But now it occurred to me that if she were right, Grant's body might soon be lined up next to Lyudmila's on the sand, and I really didn't think I could see that.

Maybe, if we were lucky, he'd just wandered off and been kidnapped again.

There was precedence. Dad and Lyudmila had a foundation, and they thought it was important to show us how the rest of the world lived. They were always taking us to Haiti or Africa or South America. As the smallest of us and the one most prone to running off, Grant made an easy target. In Sudan, I caught up with him "playing" with boy soldiers who showed him how to chop down trees with a machete. Their machetes got closer and closer to Grant's head until I paid them off with American dollars. Then there was that time in Venezuela, the express kidnapping center of the world, where Grant had learned to play Texas hold 'em and acquired a taste for guinea pig on a stick with some kind of narcotics peddlers wearing tattered uniforms with epaulets. Again: The solution had been American dollars.

I prayed that this time wasn't worse, that he hadn't been given the same treatment as Lyudmila. I'd always been able to fix him with a payoff before. I hoped I could now.

Yeah . . . denial is a powerful thing.

"Henry," Lawford said. "I need to ask you some questions. Can you understand me?"

"Yes."

"When we left the house, Pixie was with you. Where is she now?"

"Swimming in the bay."

"Why would she do a stupid thing like that?"

"No clue. I think she wanted to rule out that Grant hadn't . . . drowned, too."

Frank shook his head. "Your stepmother didn't drown, Henry. Someone just dumped her in the water to hide what they really did to her."

Lawford kicked him.

"It's all right. I have to face it sooner or later."

And that was the first time that night that I thought I might lose it. I thought of Grant and his long eyelashes and the way he jumped around so much, lighting from one interesting thing to the next, especially up here, and how you had to focus to stay with him, but it was always fun to try.

My little brother always running ahead. *Come on, Henry. Come, look.*

Here I was, sitting in the rain, with no idea what to do next.

Luckily, I was with people who did.

"All right. We'll call the sheriff. We'll get our sister out of the bay, find her dog, and get a piece of Grant's clothing. We'll find him, Henry."

"Where's Yuri?" I asked.

"We don't know," Lawford said. "And we're a little concerned about the semiautomatic shots we heard in the lagoon earlier. Those weren't random duck hunters. We're not convinced Yuri's not actually, you know, behind some of this. Maybe stay here, out of sight, till the sheriff gets here."

"Wait . . . you think *Yuri* might've killed Lyudmila? That can't be right."

There was no way. He came with her from Moscow, and I sometimes saw sweet moments between the two of them. He'd stick wildflowers in her hair, and she called him *brat* with a smile on her face. Didn't *brat* mean "brother" in Russian? I had no idea what they really were to each other. I sometimes wondered if Yuri were Lyudmila's real love and Dad just their meal ticket.

Not the time to think of that now.

"All right," Lawford said. "I'll make the calls. I'll get 911. I'll find Sammy and see about releasing Dean. Frank, try to get Pix out of the bay. Henry, for God's sake, stay here. There are already too many variables in play tonight."

I didn't think it would be too hard to get Dean out of custody, because when Dad had suggested to the sheriff that the Grays might be involved with a child's disappearance, the sheriff had laughed.

I'd seen my father issue orders before, and he made it sound as though the world would end if he didn't get what he wanted by tomorrow.

But he didn't sound as though he had half as much authority as these two did. They told me to stay put, and that was what I was going to do.

Then Pixie surfaced in the bay holding something that looked like a purple gelatinous Frisbee.

seven

PIXIE

The first death of the night I hadn't expected.

The second I was ready for.

I shouldn't have stayed swimming in the bay. I should have gotten out, found a piece of Grant's clothing, thrust it under Patience's hound nose, and let her lead the way to whatever we'd find at the end of the trail—alive, dead, injured, stranded, pecked at by an osprey and deposited in our yard.

I definitely didn't want Grant to be deposited.

But still I lingered in that cold salt water. I should've known better. The best chance I had for finding Grant alive was to start the search-and-rescue on land right away. I knew the statistics. I knew the first three hours were crucial. Who knew how much time had passed since Grant had gone missing? He had come to me at eleven that morning, asking me to carry him away. When Henry and Mr. Shepherd came to our door, it was five thirty.

But everyone other than me thought he was hiding, because that was what he did every Sunday evening. Someone was playing us—buying time to get away with something horrific we didn't entirely understand yet.

The only reason I stayed in the water was that I thought there would be a second body, and if it had somehow come free from the rowboat, I wanted to be the one to find it. Not Henry. He'd already been through enough.

So I did an inefficient thing. I stayed in the water. I flutter-kicked in a circle around the Shepherds' buoy, grasping at flotsam—and then farther out, the same thing. The water was so cold I felt it gnawing on me.

Since it was dark both above and below and I couldn't see, I "looked" with my fingers.

It was easy. Grant wasn't huge, but he was substantial enough. And there weren't any impediments in the bay—no rocks, no coral—nothing to break up the sandy bottom other than moon snails and sand dollars. Lots and lots of sand dollars. Even in this, Mr. Shepherd was rich.

At first there was nothing. Bulb kelp. Iron fixtures from some far-off unmoored ship. Razor clams. Scallop shells. *Discarded* shells—the kind from rifles, which pissed me off, but I'd learned to live with it. Even though it was illegal, hunters shot ducks in the lagoon all the time, and they occasionally got a heron, which they *deposited* for my brothers and me to take care of.

Hence the "pissed off" part.

Then something grabbed me. Gently, at first, but then more and more insistent, until it locked around my wrist and sucked at my skin at the same time.

Tentacles.

Yes, we had octopuses here. But this was no octopus. Whatever had a grip on me had fingers. That's when I heard a voice in my head saying, *Stay. Good Girl.*

Oh God. The troll. I wasn't on the shore, where I felt a measure of protection. I was in the bay. I was sure I was finally going to see the real face of the troll, just before he crunched me in half with jagged barnacle teeth.

Just the night before, I'd awoken howling because

I'd had a nightmare that he was reaching for me, just like this. Dean had splashed Clamato juice in my face, as usual, and then said, "This is getting old," before leaving me to clean up the mess.

I had not dreamed that the troll would be an active participant in this day's tragedy.

Good girl. I've come for you and everything you love. There's nothing you can do about it. Much easier if you give up and let me take you down to the wreck.

I tried to jerk my hand free, but he wasn't letting go. So I swung my leg around and stomped on his arm. Hard.

He loosened his grip enough for me to pull away.

I wanted to run screaming for the shore, but there was more than just me involved now. If Grant were still somehow floating around the bay, or had sunk to the bottom, I couldn't let the troll get him, couldn't let those sharp barnacle teeth get those little-boy bones.

I hadn't gone far when I encountered the fingers reaching for me again, insistent. Again I kicked them away.

Three times this happened.

The fourth, I found something new.

I had gotten hold of a jungle of bulb kelp and was sifting through it.

There was something there that was larger than a bulb. My fingers brushed against the thing. It wasn't solid—it was soft, as though it had been in the water a while. There was no way of knowing for sure what it was, so I opened my eyes into the darkness.

I could barely make out cloudy shapes in the flotsam I was trying to untangle, but on the bay floor, something stared back at me.

It wasn't the troll. Its eyes were gray and fathomless and set in a kind, feminine face. Not Grant, either.

Another body? Three corpses in one night? How could that be?

Then the eyes blinked. Not a corpse, but a living woman, her dark hair swirling with the ebb and flow of the tide.

I tried to grab an arm or a leg. I didn't know who— or what—she was, but I wanted to keep her from drowning if I could.

I left the tangle of flotsam and reached below me to the sand. No matter where my fingers touched, what debris I combed through, the woman's body eluded me.

My lungs felt as though they were about to explode. Surely she couldn't stay under this long? I held my breath as long as I could, grabbing at an elusive arm or anything to help the woman to the surface. But it was dark and cold, and my stored-up oxygen was exhausted, so I had to break off and come up for air before diving under again.

Still no body. Her head and her hair were the only things that seemed solid. I didn't want to pull her up by the hair, so I put one hand on either side of her face.

But when I went to pull it, it dissolved into sand and re-formed farther away from me.

I chased her. I stopped worrying about her drowning because each time that face slipped away from me and came up in a different eddy, she didn't seem to need to breathe.

What was she? This woman, whoever she was, felt so real to me, both tender and serene. I couldn't not look at her. It felt like she'd once been someone, someone I'd held dear but had forgotten.

Another wave buffeted me, and with it came a gob of flotsam. All right. Whoever this woman was, she could breathe underwater and seemed happy to stay there. But what if Grant was in this other jumble of seaweed?

I reached out for it, but before I could make contact, I felt a feathery caress on my face. The woman now had hands, and they gently stroked my cheek.

Where before she had seemed serene, now she looked sad, as though she knew what was about to happen to me but was powerless to stop it. She shook her head gently from side to side. *No.*

She didn't speak, but the message could not have been clearer. *Don't touch that, child. Let it go.*

I found it hard to breathe, not because I was underwater but because I was about to sob. How could I disappoint such a beautiful, compassionate creature?

And yet I was about to.

When the flotsam came near me again, I grabbed a piece and held on tight. I didn't know what I had. Maybe the troll. Maybe Grant. Maybe some other horrible surprise. But I grabbed anyway.

I realized now what I should've known the instant we found Lyudmila. I was wasting time. I was flutter-kicking around the shallow waters of the bay because I didn't want to face what I'd done.

Earlier, when Grant had come to me so terrified it looked like he wanted to escape his own skin, I didn't have to take him back to his house. I didn't have to ferry him across the shipping lanes, either.

I could've just done the right thing and said, "Let's go back to my place. It's chili night. My brothers and I will keep you safe."

But I didn't. Because I was afraid of what Mr. Shepherd would think.

If any one of my brothers or I pissed him off, he could build a fence so high we'd never see our beloved bay again, let alone have access to it. I would never see the herons fishing in the muck or watch osprey drop their disgusting morsels on the beach. I'd never run the sand between my toes or dig for razor clams. How would we ground ourselves, living so close to the beach but not being part of it? Without Useless Bay, my brothers and I would shrivel to nothing.

Plus Mr. Shepherd had the power to deny me access to Henry. We were supposed to be friends, he and I. But recently something had started changing between us, so now it was the kind of feeling that couldn't be fenced off. I told myself I'd never do anything to stop the way Henry looked at me now, the way his eyes lingered on the whole length of me that didn't make me feel like a too-tall freak, as though being *the Girl* weren't such a bad thing after all.

Then I did something stupid.

Which brings me to the second death in Useless Bay that night, or How I Royally Screwed Up.

At first, I thought it was just bulb kelp that I'd grabbed. And if it was a little slimy, a little elusive . . .

well, so was everything else in the bay. I had no way of knowing I'd gotten myself a live Portuguese man-o'-war, or purple jellyfish-o'-poison. The top you can brush up against with no ill effects. But the bottom? That was where the nematocysts were.

I grabbed that part of jelly and held it tight.

The second death of the night was my own.

eight

HENRY

There's a difference between seeing a dead person and watching someone die.

Pixie whipped up out of the bay with a purple gelatinous disc on her arm. She threw her hair out of her face, examined the disc, and said, "Oh, shit."

At first, I didn't understand what was going on. Frank did.

He swore and tore off down the beach, carrying his med kit, which he dropped at the tide line.

Lawford wasn't far behind. The two of them waded waist-deep into the bay and felt under the surface.

I'd never seen them in red-alert mode before. There were waves of panic rolling off them, and it was infectious.

"Have you got her?"

"Not yet."

"Come on, man. Hurry!"

"Hold on— I've got her, I've got her, I've got her!"

Once on shore, Frank rolled Pixie onto her side and whacked her hard on the back.

She barfed seawater, got to her hands and knees, and barfed more. She wiped her mouth. "I fucked up, Frank," she said.

Lawford said, "Easy there, girly man," as Frank opened his med kit.

It all happened so fast, and I was so slow. I followed them from the patio behind the main house to the beach in the cold rain and stood over them, useless. I had no idea what was going on.

Pix definitely didn't look right. Her face was as pale as a halibut, and her breathing was raspy and labored. Her whole chest drew up each time she inhaled.

I heard sirens. I told Lawford, "That'll be the ambulance. Go. It'll be faster if they know exactly where we are."

"Right," Lawford said, and he sprinted around the

house to the security gate, the lights from the motion detectors illuminating his way.

God, she looked bad. Her right arm was swelling, and with each heartbeat the swelling spread. Her fingers were already the size of kielbasas, and her face was puffed up like a French pastry.

What would happen when the swelling reached her brain? Or her lungs?

"Do something!" I barked at Frank.

"Shut up, Henry! I'm already on it!"

He pulled a yellow syringe out of his medical kit. It had the logo of a bee on it.

"Bee stings? You're treating her for a *bee sting*?"

"Not a bee. A Portuguese man-o'-war. Pix is allergic."

He jammed a needle into her thigh so hard that his sister recoiled from the force. He had to practically sit on her to keep the syringe in her flesh.

I counted to ten before he took it out, then tossed it carelessly aside. We'd worry about biohazard disposal later.

Pix shook uncontrollably. She fought for each breath.

"It's not working. *It's not working!*"

"Give it time."

"You're just spreading the poison through her faster. Look at her hands. Look at her face. Everything's puffing up."

It was true. With each heartbeat (and there were a lot of them), the evidence of the poison seemed to be spreading.

"I told you to shut up, Henry!"

"Goddamn it, Frank. Look!"

Her eyelids were so swollen they were as large as moon snails.

"Where the hell is that ambulance?" Frank shouted in Lawford's direction. Not that Lawford could hear. He was too far away.

"Frank!" I said. "It's not working!"

"Maybe you're right." He opened his med kit and took out another identical syringe and whacked her just as hard in the same spot on her leg.

This time she arched so high I was afraid her spine might break.

But that wasn't nearly as bad as what happened next.

Pix fell back onto the sand and stopped moving completely.

So did Frank.

Wait, what? Both of them? At the same time?

But there he lay, a heap of Frank, not doing anything.

I couldn't deny what was in front of me, but I didn't understand. Frank wouldn't have given up on Pixie. None of them would have ever given up on anything that wasn't yet dead.

Why the hell was he down now? Was it some kind of sympathetic quint thing? One gets hurt, the other feels the pain? Hell of a time to be too sensitive to do your job.

I shook him, but he still didn't move. I felt his carotid artery.

There was no pulse. *No pulse.*

What the hell was going on?

All right. Here were the facts: There was one me and there were two Grays. I made a choice—the kind I hoped I'd never have to make again.

I kicked Frank aside and went to work on Pixie.

I found the spot on her rib cage and started pounding on her. Hundred beats per minute. That was how often you were supposed to press down. And I thumped. And I thumped.

I don't know how long I had been keeping this up when Dad pulled me away. I screamed. "Jesus Christ, Dad! What the hell do you think you're doing?"

He wore his business face, which pissed me off. This was the wrong place to be managing anything, least of all me.

"You're in the way. You're duplicating effort."

"Yeah, well next time your girlfriend dies, I'll tell you something just as comforting."

Too late, I realized my mistake. His wife was lying dead twenty feet down the beach. The two of us sucked at interpersonal skills, and we definitely weren't huggers.

But Dad was better than me on one point. He'd gotten me out of the way. A swarm of first responders was now working on Pixie, who was so swollen she was unrecognizable.

Joyce was three paces behind my father, talking in that clipped voice into her headset, tapping on her electronic tablet. Probably to legal. "That's right. Nondisclosure statements all around. There are a lot of people involved. When the press gets ahold of this, they'll have a field day."

Meredith was there, too. "Who's that on the ground next to her, Henry? Who else are they working on?" She sounded desperate.

"I think that's Frank," I said. "Where's Sammy?"

"How should I know?" Meredith said. "We went out searching together but then split up."

Dad's face looked like putty, features that had been formed and re-formed over and over in the past hour. Finally, he said, "No sign of Grant?"

"Nothing at all. Pix has been out swimming in the bay. She should have been searching for him on land with the dog . . . ," I said. Come to think of it, where was the dog? I hadn't seen her since we were in the guard shack. "Maybe somebody should go inside and get a piece of Grant's clothing. Maybe one of her brothers can run the dog. If they're not all down."

He paid no attention to the last part. Apparently I was the only one who wondered if all the Grays had dropped at once.

"Good thinking," Dad said. "Joyce?"

Joyce pushed a button on her headset. "Mmm?" she asked Dad. "Clothing. Probably something dirty, correct?"

Dad looked to me, as though I were the search-and-rescue expert, having learned by osmosis.

"Yes," I said, because it just made sense and gave me something easier to think about than Pixie dying in front of me and her brother Frank dying at the same time for no apparent reason. I picked at the scars on my hands until I drew blood.

"Hold on, Pix, hold on!" An EMT worker was shoving another one out of the way. The first had apparently been trying to run a line in her vein and had screwed up, because a spray of blood squirted from her elbow into the air.

Interesting, interesting, I thought. *She has her own blowhole.*

Dad saw what was happening, and just like that, he became the person I needed him to be. I could see it in the slump of his shoulders, hear it in his deepening breathing. Of all the things that could have flipped him, all the tragedy that had happened and was still happening, Pixie's spurting blood was enough to make him remember I was his child.

"Don't look, son," he said, his voice full of compassion.

He pressed my face to his shoulder.

Dad wasn't usually a hugger, but that night he was. He was as damp as I was and doughy around the middle, but it was a kindness, and he didn't drip many of them on me. So I accepted.

At the same time, someone hovering over Frank shouted, "Clear!"

There was a whir and a *kerpow.*

Nothing happened.

"Look away. It's okay to look away if it's too hard. Marilyn would understand."

I sometimes forgot that Pixie's real name was Marilyn.

"I think I need to see this, Dad." And I faced her. All I could do was watch.

I'd never made her any promises, so there was nothing to be broken, but still it felt like a breach of contract, all the things we'd never get to do together flooding into my brain.

We'd known each other for years, and I just assumed we'd have time for all that stupid crap, like sitting around a campfire, eating s'mores, and listening to some guy playing acoustic guitar. The things you do on a beach, the easy way you wrap your arms around someone and hold them tight in the firelight and know that even if you don't have forever, you have this moment.

But that was always the problem with Pixie, wasn't it? We were too close. A moment wouldn't be enough.

And now it looked as though I wouldn't even get that.

Dad had told me to look away. My bad eye was still killing me from my fracas with Todd Wishlow, who thought Pix was worth only a moment.

Pixie was worth much more than that, even though I hadn't realized it until right then, when she was leaving me. She wasn't just a weekend friend. I'd known her for six years, and when you've known someone for that long and you start to think about them romantically, it automatically gets serious. And no matter how many lectures Dad gave me about getting serious too young, that was what I wanted.

I wanted the beach bonfires and someone with a guitar playing "Kum Ba Yah" and to wrap myself around her in a blanket and have her lean against me in the firelight. Rides on the Seattle Great Wheel, walking down the street with my arm around her waist, all of that.

Too late.

Dad seemed to understand and dug my hand tight into his. The most he could do was stand with me as I watched Pixie's senseless death, but he was there for me in this moment when there were all other kinds of things that needed his attention.

I loved him for it.

"Clear!"

Whir-kerpow!

No change in Frank.

"I would roll this back for you if I could, Henry," Dad said.

The man holding the paddles over Frank rocked

back onto his heels, smeared the rain on his face, and looked at his stopwatch. After a few moments, he gently closed Frank's eyes.

At the same time, whatever had worked its way through Pixie's bloodstream had gotten to where it needed to go, and she jackknifed up, and with a wheeze and a gulp she screamed and didn't stop.

Frank breathed, but he did not scream. He rolled over onto his side and started to shake. "Whoa," he said. "What happened?"

Pixie wouldn't stop screaming. Her scream was so awful it was as though she were being eaten alive. I shot away from Dad and crouched down on the beach next to her.

"Shh . . . easy, Pix. Easy. I'm here. You're all right."

"Oh my God," she said, and she bawled, her face more inflated than mine. Her eyes were still swollen shut. Both of them. She reached out blindly for anything.

I grabbed her arm and dragged her to me. "I'm here."

"I'm not ready," she said. "Please tell her I'm not ready."

"Shh . . ."

I rocked her.

She gulped air. "It's too much," she said, and gulped some more.

One of the first responders tried to pull me away. "It's okay, sir. I'm going to ask you to let us do our job now."

I told Pix once again that everything was going to be all right, but she kept crying, saying she "wasn't ready," until someone put something in her drip that calmed her down.

As they carried Pixie away on a backboard, Frank got unsteadily to his feet and said, "Whoa! That was freaky!" and the medics laughed. They didn't try very hard to carry him away as well, even though he'd been just as dead as his sister was. He was a Gray, I guess. Since he was up and acting alert, they assumed he could take it.

But I wasn't convinced that he was okay and that he didn't need to be seen by a doctor.

I wanted to know more.

Pixie and Frank dropped at exactly the same time.

I wanted to know if Dean, Sammy, and Lawford had dropped, too.

That question would have to wait.

"Son," Dad said. I'd forgotten he was there. "You can let Pixie go now."

I couldn't stop staring at Frank joking with the medics about blacking out and how, if Sammy ever found out about it, he'd never hear the end of jabs about fainting couches and smelling salts.

Who were these giants? Why did they play by different rules than the rest of us?

"Henry," Dad tried again. "Come away now. Pixie's got good people looking after her. Her long night is over. Ours is just beginning."

I turned around reluctantly. Farther up the beach at our house, a different kind of crew was walking to and from a prone form in the sand, slowly and methodically. Meredith had retreated to the patio and out of the rain.

Now that the emergency with the Grays was over, Lyudmila's death seemed to have hit my sister hard. Someone had thrown a scratchy blanket over her shoulder, and she alternately clutched it and blew her nose into it.

Behind her, the rest of our team had come out to witness the final progress of my stepmother.

Yuri wasn't there, but Joyce was talking into a headset and tapping on an electronic tablet. Our cook Hannah was wiping her hands over and over on a clean apron, and Edgar, who was still for once, had taken the baseball cap off his head and held it over his heart as a sign of respect.

I'd always liked Edgar.

Dad was trying to give me a strong smile, but it wasn't working. He hadn't bothered to put the hood up on his raincoat, and his bald head was getting pelted. As the rain dripped off his nose and down his chin, it seemed as if it was taking pieces of his face with it. He was dissolving in front of my eyes.

He was going to need my help.

This wasn't the first time we'd done this, the two men of the family protecting what was left.

I took his hand in mine. It was time to go.

nine

PIXIE

I am sitting on a log on a beach that is mine and not mine at the same time. It has all the features of Useless Bay but also possibilities that make it foreign.

A man sits next to me.

He has a long face, weather-beaten, and white hair pulled into a ponytail. He seems out of place. He wears a uniform I'm not familiar with, with a navy coat and white pants, worn but in decent repair.

Behind me, I can hear people barking orders I don't understand. Timbers groan. Something massive is back there, but I can't see it for the fog.

The keel hit bottom before the anchor did, the man sitting next to me says. He has a British accent. Upper-class.

Captain Vancouver thinks this place is useless, but I don't.

I recognize this man's profile from somewhere, a book, a display. He's someone important. I don't know how he comes to be sitting here next to me. There must be something about the fog . . .

I love gentle shores, the man says. A wonderful place for children. Much better than Deception Pass to the north. I almost didn't think we'd make it through those waters.

I know who he is.

Mr. Whidbey? I say.

He doesn't acknowledge his name, but I know it is him.

Behind us the noise continues of people trying to right the HMS Discovery. I know, without seeing it, that it has sailed into Useless Bay at low tide and that the keel has hit the sand before the anchor and now the ship is tipped to the side.

In front of us, the night is lit up red. Everyone is arrayed in front of me, as if on a stage. No one is moving. There's Lyudmila's body on the sand. There's Henry, sitting, his father wrapped around him. Meredith and Joyce hang back. There's Frank, prone, and there's another body next to his. One with long blond hair that can only be mine.

Curious.

I wish I could know you and your brothers better, Marilyn. Alas, there's little time.

You know me? You know us?

He smiles sadly but does not look at me straight on. He looks at the sea. I think he must've spent a life looking at the sea, gauging its moods.

I don't know how he knows my name or about my brothers, but I have suspicions. All I know is that I trust him. He has a trustworthy profile.

I screwed up, I say. I let Grant get away.

Hush, child, he says. It's too late for that now. She's coming.

Who's coming?

The Sea.

I know he isn't talking about the rising tide but something else.

At first, I think it's just bulb kelp rising from the bay, but then a head of human hair emerges lightly and, underneath that, a woman's face. She has features that arrange themselves into something familiar. Her clothes are tattered, and she walks with a driftwood staff, smooth and whorled, at the top of which rests a whole blue-gray Japanese fishing float.

She is beautiful.

I love her but am afraid of her at the same time. There can be no question that we are in the presence of immense power.

Who is she?

Hush, now, the man repeats.

She comes for Lyudmila first.

The Sea kneels over her empty body and caresses her white face. I can't tell if the Sea is crying or not, but she is certainly grieving. She whispers one word in Lyudmila's ear and stands to her full height. With her staff, she touches Lyudmila's dead heart.

A white light comes from within Lyudmila's chest. It illuminates the night. And then it floats away on the dark sky and is gone. And I know, somehow, that everything that Lyudmila was was contained in that light, and the body that's left lying on the beach is nothing but an empty shell.

It is now my turn.

The Sea is halfway down the sand to where my body lies, and I'm not ready for her. I'm not ready to be launched into the night the way Lyudmila was.

I'm trembling. I want the man sitting next to me to keep me safe. I reach for his hand.

Help me, I say. I'm afraid.

I can't spare you this, Marilyn. I wish I could.

The Sea is closer to my body now. Two paces away. She parts the people around me. They move aside easily. I think: Of course they do. The Sea always gets her way.

She kneels over me, where I lie thick and bloated, unable to get air, a useless thing.

Please, do something, I beg the man sitting next to me.

All we can do is pray for mercy, he says.

I don't know how. Mom never taught us.

The man grasps my hand and starts mumbling words I don't understand.

But then I see Henry's distraught profile, and I know I shouldn't pray for myself—I should pray for those I care about, and how my light winking out will affect them.

Mine shouldn't be the second bad death in one night for Henry. The first was enough. He is going to need help finding his brother, too, and I already messed up on that score.

So I start praying.

Please, I beg the beautiful woman who is bending over my body, give me mercy. I know I should've helped Grant more. I need time to atone for my mistake. And Henry needs my help. That's what I do. I find lost things.

The man sitting next to me squeezes my hand. Stay strong, Marilyn, he says. The Sea is known for her compassion. You might have a fighting chance.

The beautiful woman is crouched over my body the way she was with Lyudmila's. She taps my heart with the fishing float, but no light emerges from me.

She leans in closer and whispers one word in my ear that I cannot hear and will spend what will seem like an eternity trying to catch. It will roll toward me like foam, and roll away from me the same way.

I know I have been granted a reprieve, but with it I am being ripped away from this place as if I'm on a current.

No! Not yet! I say. I try to clutch the man's hand, but it is slipping away from me.

Take heart, Marilyn. You have a difficult path to walk. But know that I walk with you.

I wake with a jolt to the heart.

I gasp for air.

Henry is rocking me, saying it's going to be all right, but he doesn't know what's coming.

PART TWO

ten

HENRY

The sun was coming up behind us on Monday morning as Dad and I sat on the patio and answered questions. Meredith hovered, trying to get Dad to come inside. "Please, at least get warmed up and have a cup of coffee. Hannah's made a fresh pot."

"No thanks," Dad said. "I need to see this through."

"This" meant Lyudmila's body being carted away on a backboard.

Joyce hovered, too, talking into her headset. "Good news, Rupe," she told Dad. "There's a vacant plot in the cemetery where Jimi Hendrix is buried. Do you want marble or granite for the headstone?"

I failed to see how this was good news.

Dad stared blankly beyond her to the lapping waves. "You decide," he said.

"Marble, then," Joyce said. "Granite's more for kitchen counters. Do you want a particular poem or a line from a song engraved along with her name?"

Dad looked at her without really seeing her.

"Maybe something with a firebird in it," I suggested. "That was her signature dance."

"Excellent choice," Joyce said, as if I'd picked out a vintage wine. She walked off to make the arrangements.

Me? I stayed outside with Dad, almost wishing I could be as numb as he was.

Lyudmila's story may have been over, but we still had no idea what had happened to Grant, and that worried me.

There were five round scars on the palms of my hands. They were old and thick and didn't fade. Sometimes when I was under stress, like now, I picked at them. I had to content myself with levering up the skin around the edges, but if I could, I would pull back full sheets of skin and leave my hands completely raw.

Where was Grant?

It was around seven, the tide was out, and there was still no sign of my little brother. Where Dad and I sat on the patio, we were protected from the rain but not the wind. We watched people comb the beach for something worse than sand dollars.

I felt lower than the waterline.

After Lyudmila's body was taken away, we stayed there.

I tried to remind Dad that Grant had run away under worse circumstances and that we'd always gotten him back.

"Remember the boy soldiers in Sudan? Remember them? And what about that cartel in Venezuela? The fried guinea pig on a stick?"

If Dad needed cheering up, this wasn't the way to go about it. Not with his dead wife being carted away to the coroner's. He couldn't take another tragedy.

But Grant wasn't a tragedy yet, just a ticking clock. "The first few hours are critical," people in uniform kept saying, but it was a sliding scale as to what "few" meant. The last time anyone had seen Grant was when Pixie had rowed him out to the bay the day before, around eleven A.M. When we mentioned this fact to law enforcement officials, they started acting squirrelly and telling us not to give up hope.

They asked us what shoes he was wearing, as if he were a toddler swiped at Disneyland. That didn't sound right to me. Grant was ten years old and an active boy. If he were kidnapped, it wasn't going to be by someone who wanted to raise him as their own. It would be by someone who wanted lots of cash.

I thought of Lyudmila.

Maybe he had seen something he shouldn't have.

Maybe whoever it was didn't want cash. Maybe they wanted his silence.

"So we're definitely treating this as a kidnapping and not a second killing?" I asked Sheriff Lundquist. I didn't really want the answer, but I needed information.

"Right now, we're not ruling anything out," he said, which didn't seem particularly helpful. I wanted him to have at least some answers, but he didn't.

I didn't have a lot of confidence in the guy to solve a case of this magnitude. I'm sure he was a nice man, but he seemed completely overwhelmed.

And he wasn't the only one.

Dad, a man who had goals and a mission, and made sure we had our own goals and that we revisited them each year, stared blank-eyed across the water to Point No Point.

But then a man came into our lives who seemed to know what he was doing.

He was large, but not in the carved-from-the-mountains way the Grays were large. This guy had extra padding around the middle, gelled hair, and a trim mustache. He came out to the patio, flashed a badge, and introduced himself as Special Agent Wade Armstrong, FBI.

The guy did not blink. It was unsettling. I felt as though he knew every single lie I'd ever told my entire life.

I picked at my scars, digging more deeply into flesh.

He pulled up a patio chair without being invited. "I know you folks have already been through a lot. I'm sorry for your loss."

Dad nodded absently.

"But I'm going to ask you to retrace your steps one more time for me."

Dad was silent, having retreated into whatever world he was in where his wife was still alive and his three children safely accounted for.

Agent Armstrong looked to me.

"Henry, is it? How about you? Could you walk me through the timeline of yesterday between eleven and five thirty?"

"Of course," I said. "Dad was off-island at eleven. He'd forgotten a meeting. There was a kid from Rwanda in town who wanted to bring electricity to his village. It was a big photo op. 'The Kid Trying to Save Africa with Electricity.' So Dad took the helicopter to the mainland. Grant wanted to stay here, so Lyudmila and the rest of us stayed with him."

"Who else was here?"

"From the family?" I said. "Meredith. Also our travel team: Joyce, Hannah, Edgar, Yuri. Come to think of it, if you'd had a meeting, Joyce should've been with you, shouldn't she?" I asked Dad.

Dad rallied enough to act uncharacteristically cagey. "Normally, yes," he said, "but she's just been through a tough breakup. She said she wanted a few hours to walk along the beach. It's the least I could do. Joyce is my admin," Dad explained. "She never takes time off."

"I see," agent Armstrong said. "So everyone was here but you. And you came back when?"

I opened my mouth to tell him three, when I noticed something.

Twenty yards down the beach, one of the Gray brothers stopped inspecting the beach, stood up, and looked toward the lagoon.

Fifty yards away, another Gray did the same thing, as if some kind of sonar had pinged him.

The two Grays started running toward the lagoon.

"Something's happening," I said, and took off after them.

I sprinted down the patio and around the house.

There was a bunch of people crowded behind a police cordon at the edge of our property. As soon as they saw me, the questions started flying like bottle rockets. "Henry! Over here! Henry! Do you care to comment?" I heard the word *lies*. I heard the name *Marilyn*. I heard the word *diet*, or maybe just the word *die*.

I stopped at the trailhead that led to the path through the lagoon. Where were the Gray brothers? It wasn't like they were easy to miss.

There. All four of them were down in the lagoon itself, waist-deep in the muck. I hadn't seen them at first because their hair looked like beach grass. I ran down the trail and parted the branches of the Scotch broom, afraid of what I'd see.

I looked closer. The muck itself wasn't all brown. Parts of it were tinted red. They were examining something that was floating. From the tilt of their heads, I could tell it wasn't good. This wasn't their "Interesting

. . . a bird of prey dropped a spiny dogfish" head tilt. This was much, much worse.

Oh no. I wanted to look away, but I couldn't. This was no horror movie. This was real. They had my brother down there, and he was so bad off that Frank wasn't even trying to revive him.

"Dean?" I asked softly.

One of the four heads shot up.

"You don't need to see this, Henry," Dean said.

I was tired of hearing that.

There was no easy path down, just rocks covered with barnacles. Finally, I got down on my butt and slipped down, tearing my jeans and skin. Soon I was waist-deep in the muck with them.

"What is it?"

The thing they were looking at was Grant's size, but not his shape. There was a long, floppy ear, and there was a paw, but the body was practically unrecogniz- able, it was so riddled with holes. Those holes weren't even well placed along the body. It was just one great big spray of them, letting out blood and intestines and jellied eyes.

This gory, perforated rag was all that was left of Patience.

"Jesus," I said, sick and relieved at the same time.

"You really didn't need to see this. You've already got enough to deal with," one of them said. I was almost positive it was Dean, because he was usually the first to respond when they were in a group—a trait that had landed him in the Island County sheriff's office the night before.

"Jesus. I don't know how we're going to tell Pix," another said. Sammy. You could see part of a scar along his hairline. He had a bad motocross accident a couple of years ago that nearly killed him.

I looked at the rag with holes that used to be Pixie's pet. I should've been more shocked, I suppose, but after the night I'd had, and given the state she was in, it was like looking at roadkill.

"Who would do this?" I said, more to myself than the Grays.

"Someone who didn't want to be found," said a voice from the trail above us.

I looked up to the dike. I was so caught up in the Grays' drama, it hadn't occurred to me I was being followed. But there was agent Armstrong, standing in a black raincoat, looking ready to unleash a whole lot of fury on whatever sick whack job had reduced Patience to a pile of holes.

He'd remembered a piece I'd forgotten. Patience

was the best scent hound in the state. If you didn't want her on your trail, this was one way to get rid of her.

As the rest of us stood there, wallowing, I noticed that agent Armstrong didn't bother to climb down and get into the muck with us. He didn't need to. He had perfect command of the situation from above.

eleven

PIXIE

Mom stayed with me the first two hours of my incarceration—I mean, my *recovery*—at Whidbey General Hospital in Coupeville, but she left when the swelling went down and my face returned to its natural size. The tests had all been run, my chest hooked up to wires and monitors, and now we were just waiting for the results. Although she wanted to help find Grant as much as I did, she was reluctant to leave.

"I don't think you understand what you put me through, Marilyn. You had to be *resuscitated*. That's a first. I almost prayed when I found out what had happened to you."

"It was an accident."

"Don't give me that shit. You're my only girl. And as such, I hold you to higher standards than the rest. That includes not getting poisoned. Your face is looking a little better."

I reassured her that I felt fine, and finally she left to make coffee and sandwiches for the people searching for Grant.

"All right. I'll go. But only because you've got more sense than some of your brothers, and there's work to be done. You'll call me when the doctors come back with your prognosis?"

I told her I would. I told her I felt fine. I did not tell her that I felt *normal*.

The truth was, I was scared of what the brain scans would turn up. I was sure that at least part of my brain had turned to jelly, and I wanted to put off Mom's reaction to it as long as possible.

After all, nobody with a *normal* brain would've seen what I saw the night before: the man sitting on the log . . . the woman coming from the sea . . . Lyudmila becoming an incandescent light. And then the woman standing over me, whispering something in my ear, something important that, try as I might, I couldn't remember.

I closed my eyes and tried to remember but couldn't tune out the beeping from the machines I was hooked up to. What had she said?

After a while, I gave up trying and focused on the wall-mounted TV. I watched the manhunt for Grant Shepherd, the one that Patience and I should've wrapped up by now.

The news listed Yuri Andreevich Bulgakov as a "person of interest." Everybody liked him for Lyudmila's murder *and* Grant's disappearance. His motive was supposed to be money.

Nobody had seen him since Sunday afternoon. The newscasters hinted he might have a link to the Russian mafia, which pissed me off. I mean, just because he was Russian didn't mean he was carrying out hits on people. True, he owned that Kalashnikov, but I figured that was more out of habit than anything else.

Yuri was just too *sad*. When he was off duty and dipping into the cornichons and the vodka, he would stare a little too long at the big house and start singing verses of Russian folk songs. He would get a faraway look, massage Patience's wrinkles, then turn to Henry and me and say, "Ah, to be young and in love."

He loved Lyudmila with a doomed, Russian kind of love.

I always assumed that was enough for him.

I didn't know where he'd gone, but I hoped he was okay.

I had been lying in my bed in the ER for about seven hours when Sammy showed up.

"Sammy, thank God. Have you guys found Grant yet?"

He shook his head no. His face had a weight to it I'd never seen before, and I knew at once that it was bad news.

"I need to tell you about Patience," he said.

He handed me a bag of clean clothes. Then he sat with me and waited for the results of the MRI. As he did, he recited the facts.

"Whoever did it used the Kalashnikov, Pix. Remember? Yuri's gun? We know it was that weapon because of the caliber of the bullet. They still haven't recovered the gun yet, but it's only a matter of time.

"Whoever did it would've shot her at close range. The first bullet would've made her jump. You remember how vocal she was? There would've been a great big *aroo*. But she wouldn't have felt the other thirty-two.

Thirty-three bullets total, Pix. *Thirty-three.* That's some seriously twisted shit right there."

I know not all brothers are like this. Some might have said she wouldn't have felt a thing or gone on about burying her under the azaleas that would bloom lovely and pink in the summertime, like that shit would've consoled me.

But not my Sammy. Sammy was all about statistics and records. So he counted the bullets. He told me the facts. He let me draw my own grim conclusions.

Sammy had no way of knowing my part in all this. That *I'd* hidden the Kalashnikov when Henry and I had been alone searching the guard shack for Yuri and clues to where Grant had gone. I remembered how big the gun had been and how I hadn't wanted it lying around where anyone could swipe it and use it on some little kid. That gun had scared me, so I stashed it out of sight in the Scotch broom.

But the fact that it had been found and used meant that someone had been watching us—had been watching *me.*

The night before, when we'd fanned out to look for Grant, we'd all been in a position to be picked off by that Kalashnikov one by one—Lawford, Frank, Henry, me—who knows how many more.

But no. Whoever had been watching us had deliberately taken out the dog—the one with the well-trained, professional nose.

I didn't know what that meant, but I was going to find out. And when I did, I was going to shoot the bastard who did it with thirty-three slugs myself.

That's how I felt like mourning.

twelve

HENRY

I was right about agent Armstrong. After we found what was left of Pixie's dog, things started happening.

He began to notice what we hadn't, the first of which was to wonder why, when we'd searched the house and the garage and even the guard shack, no one had thought to search the Breakers.

"The Breakers is shut tight," Dad told him. "The only time we open it is if we have guests. And we haven't had any in months."

"What if Grant wanted to play hide-and-seek

there?" I suggested, mostly to myself, but agent Armstrong seized on the idea.

"Let's open it up and take a look around," he said.

"Okay," Dad said. "But I don't see why. Grant doesn't hide unless one of the Grays is abetting him. Usually at their house."

"That's not true," Meredith said. "He likes small places. He likes spots where he can be alone with his book of Russian fairy tales."

I hadn't even realized Meredith was with us at the time. We were standing on the patio, facing the bay, getting buffeted by the wind and rain.

I should've known things would change for Meredith with Lyudmila gone. They would be different for all of us, but for Mere especially.

Mine wasn't the only family to have a boys' team and a girls' team. While Lyudmila was around, Meredith mostly spent time with her. Mere usually talked to Dad and me only at the dinner table to make sure we were all well versed on the issues of the day. Sometimes talking to Lyudmila and Mere was like talking to a foreign species. We didn't understand why they needed to spend $98 on yoga pants in slightly different accent colors. Black with a purple waist. Black with a pink waist. Black with a red waist. Now that there was no

Lyudmila, Meredith had two choices: spend time with us or spend time with her phone.

Even odds.

And it turned out that she was right about Grant and small spaces and the Breakers, because when agent Armstrong turned the knob on the door to the cottage, it was unlocked. There were many possible reasons for it, but I liked Mere's the best. Private spaces. Some place to curl up alone and read Russian fairy tales.

"Stay back," agent Armstrong said, and he took the safety off his gun as he went through the door, Sheriff Lundquist following closely behind.

Dad and Mere and I stood outside, anxious, getting drenched, wondering what they'd find.

The two of them were inside a long time. When agent Armstrong came out, he said to the other cops, "Can we get eyes in here?"

"What's going on?" Dad demanded, charging to the entrance. "Is it my son? Oh my God, *is it Grant?* Can I see him?"

"Calm down, Mr. Shepherd," agent Armstrong reassured him. "He's not here. But I think we may have found a crime scene . . . Henry, why don't you take your father back to the house. Make sure he gets a shower. Something to eat. It's been a long night."

"What kind of crime scene?" Dad said. "I demand to know. You're on my property."

Dad had reverted to landowner bully, the way he was when he first met the Grays. I didn't like him when he was like this. He was an asshole.

Agent Armstrong wasn't fazed. "There's a rug that appears to be missing and signs of a struggle. I need a team to go over it. In the meantime, the best thing you can do to help is take care of yourself. We'll notify you when we know something more. It's best if you go back to the house for now."

Mere and I looked at each other.

"Come on, Dad," Mere said, and he let her take his arm and lead him away.

I followed, looking over my shoulder as person after person went into the Breakers, carrying kits and putting on booties. They looked like they knew what they were doing. I just hoped they would find some bit of something that hadn't been bleached.

In the main house, I stationed myself by a window in the upstairs hallway. Edgar came by every so often with green tea and gingersnaps from Hannah. I watched people come and go from the Breakers.

I should've known. It was the closest building to

the bay. The door practically backed right onto the seawall. All someone would have to do was heave Lyudmila's body over into the rowboat and dump her into the water.

I saw agent Armstrong leave the Breakers and make his way up the driveway toward our house.

I ran downstairs and practically tripped over Meredith as I did. I wasn't the only one keeping an eye on the investigation.

Was it me? Or was there something about the way Mere looked at me and then avoided my gaze? She'd given me that same shifty look when she'd been going out with Ajay Wijenaike, a guy from the crew team and one of Todd Wishlow's best friends. It's not that I minded that she went out with someone from the team, but Ajay and Todd were pieces of work who were only interested in our money. She knew it; I knew it. She dated Ajay anyway.

Now I was sure she had done something else that she knew I wouldn't approve of. And she'd done it recently.

But agent Armstrong was downstairs and probably had news, so I decided to put off asking her about it.

Big mistake.

• • •

Agent Armstrong was already in the living room when Mere and I came crashing in.

"... pursuing other lines of inquiry at the same time. When was the last time anyone saw Yuri Bulgakov?"

"Yuri? I don't know. No one's found him yet. He came to the island with the travel team, didn't he, Joyce?"

Joyce was sitting in the corner, as usual, making notes on her electronic tablet. "Actually, he came to the island *before* the family arrived to make sure everything was ready. I saw him in the guard shack myself when we got here Friday evening."

"And is he in the habit of carrying semiautomatic firearms and shooting dogs with them?"

"The first part, yes. The second part? No," I said before Dad had a chance to answer.

Joyce scowled at me. I'd spoken out of turn. This was a serious breach of etiquette. Since she used to be our nanny, she thought she could still make us behave with a look. For the most part, she was right. But Dad was tired, and there was no way that Yuri would be plugging dogs. Especially not Patience, whom he helped train.

"I see," agent Armstrong said as Meredith and I sat down on the couch on either side of Dad. "Could you

please tell me the exact nature of the relationship of this man with your late wife?"

Dad looked startled. "What are you talking about? They were close. Friends from Russia."

"How close?"

"Brother-and-sister close. My wife, she didn't have the best home situation growing up in Moscow. Her father was an abusive alcoholic. I get the feeling that Yuri saved her from that somehow. He got her away from her father and into the ballet academy. At least, that's what she told me. All I really know is that she wouldn't come to the States without him."

"She called him *brat*," Mere said. "That means 'brother,' right?"

"But they weren't real brother and sister," I said. "It was a more spiritual thing."

Agent Armstrong said, "They weren't directly related. Which you would know if you had done a thorough background on him before you installed him as head of security."

Dad gnashed his teeth. Not a good sign. "Joyce?" he said.

She bit her lip. She was in trouble. I didn't know that she could get defensive. I *did* know that she'd had a bad week. Something about a breakup with her latest boyfriend? "Well, I wasn't exactly sure how to do it, was I? Being your admin was still new to me. I'd like to see *you* wade through Russian bureaucracy." She put down her tablet and rubbed the bridge of her nose. "I'm sorry. Forgive me. It was a long time ago. You wanted to know if he had been a member of the Russian military. The truth is, I had no idea how to find out. I wanted to do a good job, but at the time you *had* to be with Lyudmila, and Lyudmila wasn't going anywhere without Yuri. You said to make it happen. So I did. He's been a diligent worker. Very protective of the family. Never absent. Never late."

"Until yesterday," Mere said.

"What are you suggesting, agent Armstrong?" Dad said.

"I'm saying that our background checks have turned up the fact that he not only was a member of the Russian military, he was a member of Russian homeland security."

"He was a *spy*?" I said. If it hadn't been such a miserable weekend, I would've thought that was cool.

Agent Armstrong went on. "I'm also saying that perhaps his relationship with your wife wasn't as innocent as it seemed. That maybe they had a rendezvous at the Breakers while you were on the mainland. That maybe they quarreled and it got out of hand and he strangled her."

I couldn't believe it. Yuri, with the three-day stubble and the bags under his eyes. Yes, he loved her, but he never would've tried to get close to her. He was too tragic for that kind of thing. "You and me, Henry, we understand love from afar a little too well, I think," he said on more than one occasion when he caught me looking at Pixie, the whole long length of her. "My chances are over, but you can still play a hand. Why not ask her on a real date? Flowers. Candy."

"No," I said now, and Joyce shot me another glare. "Yuri would never have made a move on Lyudmila, and he certainly wouldn't have strangled her."

"But his weapon killed the best scent hound in the state," agent Armstrong said. "And the man himself is nowhere to be found. I'd like to talk to him directly."

"Henry," Mere said. "You've got to admit it looks grim."

She was right. All the same, I couldn't help thinking Yuri would find something philosophical about it.

Ah . . . death. Such a tragedy. Such a beautiful woman. You never know what life brings you. That is why you must tell your girl what you think of her before it is too late.

thirteen

PIXIE

It was late afternoon when I got home. In the backyard, Dean was digging a hole toward the end of the bluff, away from the Douglas firs, closer to the scrub, the ironwood, and the Himalayan blackberries, where all the critters made their homes. Next to him was a large object wrapped in an old blanket that was stained red.

I grabbed another shovel from the garage and went out to join him. After all, she was *my* dog.

"You don't need to help me, Pix. You just got out of the hospital," Dean said, looking up.

We were in the hospital so much, the house rule was that we had twenty-four hours to rest after after we were discharged. But the reality was that no one rested without being called a wuss. It wasn't worth the grief. But Dean was talking about something else. He was talking about burying Patience. He had his rain poncho on and his mud boots. It was a torrential day. Everything was getting blasted in the wind and sideways rain.

"Yes, I do."

It didn't go quickly. Even away from the trees, the roots were thick, and even though our arms were thicker, it was slow going, and we had to bury her deep because some of the critters that made their homes in the brush were coyotes. We didn't want Patience dug up and carried off.

From where we worked, we could see the Shepherd McMansion below. It was swarming with activity. Helicopters circled overhead; Coast Guard boats got as close to shore as they could, which wasn't close. Volunteers walked the lagoon; three of my brothers among them. They were taking it so slow they looked like herons.

I didn't forget my obligation to the Shepherds. Henry texted me more than once to come down and show him how to walk the grid, but I told him that Sammy could help him. I knew I couldn't compare the loss of a dog to the loss of a stepmother, but I wanted to honor Patience, who'd been a menace but also a hero.

I hadn't realized how heavy Patience was until Dean and I both heaved her into the deep hole we'd dug. We had to swing her to get her to the bottom. Dean had done his best to wrap her in an old blanket, but the red blood kept seeping through. Her tongue lolled out and got dirty, but she didn't care.

That was when I knew that Patience was finally, completely gone. All that was left were memories and compost.

fourteen

HENRY

gent Armstrong wanted us to stay indoors and wait for news, but I wasn't so good at that. I had to know what had happened to Grant—even if it was the worst thing I could think of. I'd been mentally preparing myself for it ever since Pixie and I turned over the rowboat the night before. At the very least, I wanted to "walk the grid" the way the Grays were doing.

Pix was back from the hospital. Sammy said she was okay and all her tests had come back normal. I could see her at the edge of her yard on top of the bluff, working at something. I texted her to come down and show me what to look for when walking a grid, and she texted back that she couldn't at the moment, that she was burying her dog. But she'd ask one of her brothers to break off from where they were searching the lagoon. That one of them would help me. *Break off?* I texted her. *Should they do that?*

She called me—not a text, an actual call—and told me not to worry. There was plenty of manpower, and she was sure I must be going stir-crazy without a job to focus on. Sammy was on his way.

I watched her from a distance as she talked. Her speech was punctuated by grunts, I realized, because she was shoveling dirt.

I looked at the lagoon separating her house from mine. All that muck. Dad had wanted to fence it. When we'd first bought this house, before we knew the Grays, he wanted to build a barrier so they couldn't get through. Not to the lagoon, not to the bay, both of which were legally ours.

And now I thought of what a mistake that would've been. Both to keep the Grays out of their natural habitat and to put a fence between us. Now we were so intertwined I wasn't sure where the Shepherds ended and the Grays began.

We were lucky that Grant had stumbled onto the Grays six years ago and that they were the kind of kids who liked looking after him, who played hide-and-seek with him, who enjoyed showing him gross and interesting things, such as how the guts of spiny dogfish were so disgusting not even scavenger birds would eat them.

They must've been like characters out of one of Grant's fairy-tale books. Of course he'd want to be by them.

Once upon a time there was a curious little boy who strayed away from his mother and father and ran into five friendly giants walking down a bluff.

We will show you treasures, they said.

I have enough treasure, the little boy replied.

Not like this.

Without the Grays, Dad might have toyed with our weekend house as he did his other assets, fenced it, got tired of it, and moved on after a year or two to some other playground.

Now, no matter what had happened, it was still our refuge.

• • •

I made my way outside to meet Sammy when he came and stumbled onto the arrival of the *second*-best scent hound in the state.

Sheriff Lundquist was at the gate to the shore road and waved through a truck with a huge bed that had the logo of a ram in front and a large crate in the back.

Meredith came outside, too. Apparently, she was no better at staying put than I was.

The sheriff was greeting the driver. "Thanks for coming, Dan. I know it's a long way from Bremerton."

"No problem, Sheriff. Tonka and I are happy to help. It's been a long time since we've gotten called to the island."

"No need till now," Sheriff Lundquist said with a half chortle. And I knew why. He was proud. Patience belonged to the whole island, the way the quints did. Everyone shared in their glory and hard work, and condoled with them when their work turned up remains and not live bodies.

And now they had to resort to calling in someone off-island for assistance. It was like asking someone from a different school to the prom.

"I was real sorry to hear about Patience," Dan said. "I never thought that dog would come to anything. But she and that big gal sure proved me wrong."

Big gal? Big gal? He was talking about Pixie. *Give me an oar. I'm gonna hurt him.*

Meredith seemed to sense what I was thinking and dug her fingernails into my arm, reminding me that I'd already broken one clavicle this week, thank you very much.

After a certain amount of pain, I realized that Dan-whoever-he-was-in-the-down-vest had a beast that could help us find Grant, so I kept my trap shut.

Mere may have made me behave, but I could tell by the way she bit her lip that she was as skeptical as I was about the abilities of the animal named Tonka.

The beast hopped out of the crate, and we saw he was twice the size of Patience, with his balls still intact and swinging, of course. The first thing he did was pee on a tire of the giant truck, showing off his giant penis and copious amounts of urine. The message was clear: Dan in the Down Vest was compensating for something. We had a hard time taking him and his dog seriously, which may have colored what happened later.

Dad came out of the house with one of Grant's shirts. After many handshakes and politenesses of "I'm real sorry for your troubles," Dan thrust the shirt under the beast's snout. Tonka put his nose to the ground and went straight to the garage, then he pawed at the door until we opened it. He galumphed to a spot by a pile of cable that had some blankets piled into what looked like a nest.

The blankets were just the kind we threw over the rowboat and the kayaks, but they'd been arranged in a way to seem comfy. Under different circumstances, I wouldn't have minded curling up in those and taking a nap. I loved the places where we hung up the boats. To me, they smelled of early-morning mists rising off the water and staph infections from dirty oars. Nirvana.

Tonka sniffed around for a while, then the beast walked nose-down back out of the garage and to the gate, where he stopped and looked stupidly up and down the street that led along the shore.

There was no *aroo* sound.

There was no more sniffing.

The trail was cold.

Sammy had emerged from the lagoon at this point. He came up to where Dad and Mere and I were standing mutely, watching Tonka do nothing.

He broke the silence. "What's going on? They brought in *Tonka*?" he said, as if he couldn't believe that anyone were so desperate.

I said what we were all thinking. "That dog is a moron."

"He's not a moron, actually," Sammy said. "He's just a male, so he pees on everything he sniffs."

Mere rubbed the bridge of her nose. "Total moron."

She smiled slyly and exchanged a look with Sammy that lasted a little too long.

I glanced at Meredith, and she quickly looked away. Was I imagining things, or was something going on between those two?

"Look, whether or not the dog is a moron, it's obvious the trail ends here, on the shore road," Dad said.

"So if we believe the dog, Grant got into a car, right?" I said. "We can call in the people walking the grid and trolling the bay and issue an Amber Alert."

"Wait just a second. Have we thought that maybe he went willingly with someone and that maybe he's safe?" Mere suggested. "He went willingly with Pixie in the rowboat."

It was common knowledge by now. Pixie hadn't been in good enough shape to tell everyone last night, so I told them that she was the one who had taken Grant out. Then, when she got home from the hospital, she told the sheriff everything she remembered.

"He's a minor, and whoever took him didn't have my consent," Dad said. "So it's a kidnapping. Even if that someone was a Gray. And I will prosecute whoever took him to the full extent of the law." He glared at Sammy.

"Whoa," Sammy said, backing up. He had come here to help us out and instead was getting a fight from a man whose wife had just died, so that put him in a position where he couldn't defend himself.

"Dad," I said, "you can't think after all this shit that they're still playing . . ."

It was right then, when we were standing in the drive arguing, paying no attention to what was going on around us, that the second-best scent hound in Washington State began to bay.

fifteen
PIXIE

When we finally filled Patience's grave, Dean marked the spot with a stick. Not a cross, because Mom would have yanked it out of the ground and winged it into the lagoon.

So a stick.

He asked me if I wanted to say a few words.

I said what was expected of me. "Patience. You ate Shih Tzus. And goose poop. But you found things." I stopped. I remembered that first day, bicycling back from my brothers, the last child, the one whose only superpower was that she was *the Girl*. But how, after

I started working with Patience, I had gotten a reputation for being a finder of lost things—a reputation my brothers didn't quite share, even though they were keen to help out.

I thought of her trembling that first day, the way she crept out of her crate, and how I had to keep her from howling, and how it gave me a purpose that I hadn't had before. "You found me," I finally said. "So thank you."

Dean tamped down the dirt with his shovel a little better, and I looked around. With Patience, I knew what to do. Without her, now what?

"That's that, then," Dean said, wiping the rain across his face. Drips of water hung from his nose. Mine as well, I was sure.

And then it happened. One of those weird moments that told me, no matter what the doctor said, I wasn't *normal*. Not after what had happened in the bay and when I came out of it.

There. Under the eaves of our house.

I saw Patience. Alive. Not when I was looking at her directly, but out of the corner of my eye. She was sitting calmly beside the house under my bedroom window, in a patch of ivy. When I looked at her straight on, she wasn't there. But when I looked at something else, anything else, there she was again, lounging, completely dry in the downpour.

"You go on down to the Shepherds', Dean," I said. "I need a moment alone."

Dean nodded. "I understand. Don't take too long. Even without Patience, we're all still looking to you. You're still the finder."

I tried to tell him this wasn't true, that I'd lost everything when I'd lost Patience, but he was Dean, and Dean didn't lie.

Still, I needed time to investigate something I couldn't explain to him. So as soon as he was out of sight, I tried looking at the ghost of my dead dog again. I trained my eyes in the distance away from the house, and there she was, under my bedroom window, calmly sitting, but when I looked at her full on, she disappeared, like an optical illusion.

What was going on?

I walked in the direction I'd seen Patience. There was nothing on the ground where I'd seen her. A small depression in the ivy, but nothing large enough to indicate 150 pounds of dog had just been there. My bedroom window was wide open. The screen had been peeled back, and inside it was too dark to see. One thing was for sure: My bedroom was getting flooded, and I couldn't shut the window from outside. I didn't know what kind of critter could've done such damage. Maybe Sammy was playing a prank on me? But Sammy was walking the lagoon.

So I went around the house and through the garage, dumped my muddy boots and my parka, then made my way to the bedroom.

The cold was the first thing I noticed, not the man with a semiautomatic rifle.

"I did not kill her."

"Jesus Christ! Yuri?"

I flipped on the overhead light to get a better look.

He was drenched and muddy and sitting on my bed, tightly gripping his Kalashnikov with both hands. He looked as though he hadn't slept in a week, and his eyes kept darting around me to the hallway.

"Off, please," he said.

I switched off the light, but I could see his outline in the dark, and more later as my eyes grew accustomed to the dimness.

"You will also please keep your voice down and close the door behind you. I need to explain some things."

"Fine. Fine. Just put the gun down. Did you shoot my dog?"

That was the least of the crimes he'd committed if he'd committed them, but it seemed important. After all, he helped me train her.

"Are you not listening? I did not shoot anybody. I did not shoot Patience. Patience was good dog."

"Then where did you find your gun? I hid it in the Scotch broom last night."

"You are a very silly girl. Do you not know you were being watched? We were all being watched. All the time."

He pointed to his eye with one hand and kept a tight grip on his Kalashnikov with the other. "Me, I thought it was different. I thought that I was doing the watching. But I have been outspied. For many years."

"What do you mean? Who outspied you?"

The door burst open. Dean was at my shoulder. I was trying to be quiet and do everything Yuri said, but I should've known that one of my brothers would be coming to check on me after I just buried my dog. Lawford, Sammy, and Frank were probably on their way, too.

"Yuri, buddy. Put the gun down," Dean said.

"Jesus Christ, Dean, get out of here. I've got it under control."

There was baying in the distance. I knew it wasn't from a ghost dog. My dog would not hunt this man no matter what shape she was in. No, whatever dog was coming our way was alive.

Time. We needed time. I wanted to hear what he had to say.

"You do not belong here, little boy," Yuri said. "This is a private conversation between Marilyn and myself. I need to tell her something important before I die."

"Whoa, whoa, whoa. Nobody else has to die here today," I said. "Believe me. I tried it last night. It isn't what it's cracked up to be."

"Where's Grant?" Dean said.

"I do not know where Grant is. Somebody has hidden him. I think it's for the best. Marilyn, there are many things at stake now, yes?"

"Yes, Yuri. Many things. Put down the gun, and we'll talk about them."

"Do you not understand? I will try to explain . . ." He waved the gun toward my closet. There was a *snip* sound, and I was facedown on the carpet with a heavy weight on top of me.

Then a lot of voices. One deep one saying, "Who took the shot?" over and over again. "I wanna know who took that shot!"

The weight let up. I heard someone else say, "Stay down," and another person say, "Clear."

I didn't understand what was going on. I didn't understand that my eyes had been shut tight until I opened them and saw Yuri sprawled on my bed, a neat hole in the middle of his head, leaking blood and other matter I would discover later on my comforter and sheets and mattress.

"Frank! Someone call Frank!" I said.

Even as I said it, I knew there was nothing Frank could do.

Yuri was dead. It had all happened so quickly and so neatly. I hoped the tattered woman with the staff would find him and release his light into the world.

It was too late for anyone else to help.

sixteen

HENRY

We were so busy arguing, we hadn't realized that agent Armstrong had already given Dan in the Down Vest another item for Tonka to sniff—this one not belonging to Grant. They were changing the focus of their search from Grant to Yuri.

We didn't find this out until later. All we knew now was that Tonka was running, howling up the dark path to the Grays' house, and Dad was muttering all the time, "I knew it. I knew you were hiding him."

"Grant's not there," Sammy tried to tell us. "This is something else."

The FBI and the sheriff were running as well, and they were outpacing us. A couple of them asked us to stay behind them.

When he got to the base of the bluff, Tonka broke off from the main trail and picked his way up a rarely used path through the blackberries. This path emerged in the Grays' backyard. The FBI and Sheriff Lundquist followed close behind.

There was no space for Dad, Mere, Sammy, and me, so we took the regular trail that led to their front yard.

We were halfway up the drive when I heard the shot.

Oh no . . . Pixie!

I sprinted faster.

I was the first in the front door.

"What's happened?" I said. "Is Pixie all right?"

Pix was sitting on the sofa, with Mrs. Gray draped around her. "We've had a shock, Henry."

Dad came in, out of breath. "Where's Grant?"

Mrs. Gray looked confused, as though there were only so much she could process, and right now it was all about her youngest, her only girl.

"I don't think this is about Grant, Dad," I said, although I still wasn't quite sure myself.

Pixie's giant brothers were standing shell-shocked around the living room.

Dean finally said, "It was your guard. He was in Pixie's room. He had a gun. The police took him down. It was so fast . . . Jesus, it was fast."

Mere was standing next to me, and her shoulders began to heave. She seemed to understand what had happened before the rest of us did. "Yuri's been shot? But he didn't deserve it! He wasn't a threat. He was just a sad, old guy."

Her cries became torrential. Sammy put an arm around her shoulder. He did it gingerly, as though he were breaking a taboo. "You don't need to be here for this, Mere. Mr. Shepherd, why don't I take her home?"

Dad nodded, looking vacant. "I thought they'd found my son."

Mrs. Gray, with her arm still around Pixie's shoulder, said, "I'm sorry, Rupe. I'll make us some coffee. It's going to be another long night."

She ran a hand through her daughter's hair, gave her a soft look that Pix didn't catch, then got up and went to the kitchen.

I'd never seen Mrs. Gray look so grateful. It occurred to me that she might, just might, have a favorite child.

Or maybe she'd be this relieved if any of them had survived being held at gunpoint.

Dad didn't stay long, but I did—mostly hanging back, hoping nobody would kick me out before I heard Pix explain what had happened with Yuri. I owed Yuri that much.

Agent Armstrong sat on the love seat in the living room and drank cup after cup of coffee as he asked Pixie questions.

His face was a thunderclap. Yuri had been shot too soon—before there was any chance for him to be interrogated. And now the investigation had been bungled. He was trying not to show his disappointment to Pixie, but I guessed that later someone was going to get his ass handed to him.

"He said he didn't know where Grant was," Pixie was saying. "He said that somebody had hidden him and that it was for the best."

"Can you remember anything else he said? Anything at all?"

"Yes. I don't think he took Grant or killed Lyudmila. He called me silly. He said he had been 'outspied.'"

"Outspied?"

"Yes. That was his word."

As they wheeled Yuri's body out on a stretcher, Mrs. Gray handed out peach cobbler to anyone who wanted it.

"Can you think of any reason why Mr. Bulgakov would come to you for help?" he said.

"Yes," Pix said, shivering beneath her blanket. "He helped me train my dog."

"The bloodhound? The one that was killed with his weapon?"

"That's the one. We spent a lot of time together training Patience. She needed a lot of work. The guy who was originally supposed to train her half-assed the job. Yuri helped me fix her."

There seemed to be something going on with Pixie's eyes, because she wouldn't look at agent Armstrong straight on. She kept looking at the floor. Maybe she was just tired.

"So you think maybe Mr. Bulgakov came to explain why he killed your dog?"

"I think he came to explain that he *didn't* kill Patience, and he wanted to tell me who did. I don't think he killed Mrs. Shepherd, either. I think he wanted to set me straight on that. But he didn't have the chance."

Agent Armstrong glared at Sheriff Lundquist, whose expression didn't change.

So we all knew who had been quick on the trigger. And now, thanks to the good sheriff, we were no closer to the truth or to finding my little brother. The information had stopped.

I wanted to blame him, but if I had found someone threatening Pixie, I might've done the same thing.

Agent Armstrong was still talking. "And Mr. Bulgakov gave no indication who this person might be. The one who outspied him."

Pixie shook her head. "None whatsoever."

Agent Armstrong asked Pixie more questions about what had happened the day before, and she answered them. But something was stuck in my mind after Pixie had said the word *outspied*.

The CCTV had been stuck on a loop showing the Breakers, but why in the garage, too? What had been going on there? Had Grant gone to the nest of blankets before he went to the gate? What had happened in the garage that he'd known about that someone would want covered up?

We were down to a short list of people who had the capability to find Lyudmila in the Breakers when Dad was away: There were the Grays, and our family. And then there was our travel team: Hannah, our cook; Edgar, who stayed above the garage; Joyce, who thought she was so important she was always just a step behind Dad; and Yuri, who was dead. One of us was a killer.

No wonder Grant didn't want to come home when Pixie rowed him into the Sound. He was a witness. He'd seen something happen to his own mother, and he'd told no one. Not even me.

I swear, as soon as I found the little urchin, I was going to kick his ass for not coming to me first.

If I found him.

Outside, the weather was picking up. The wind whistled through the cracks in the windows, and the rain splashed against the glass.

I wove my way across the room and found myself sitting next to Pixie on the sofa. Agent Armstrong had finished his questioning and left with the others. Without thinking, I took her hand. I interlocked my fingers in hers. She took it and squeezed.

I should've known better than to reach for her.

Pixie was an observant girl.

She felt my scars. I'd been picking at them again. I couldn't leave them alone, especially when I was stressed. She opened my palm and counted them. Five. A whole constellation of old cigarette burns.

"They're bad again, aren't they?" she said.

"It's been a long couple of days," I said.

She'd seen the scars before. Most of the time, they were easy to overlook.

But now they were leaking, oozing red.

Pix got up, went to the bathroom, and came back with a first aid kit. As she dabbed at my hand with neomycin ointment, branches blew back and forth against the windowpanes. Something swooped overhead, and I didn't ask what.

"These aren't ever going to fade, are they, Henry?" Pix asked, investigating my skin.

And maybe it was the trauma of the past couple of days, or the idea that I might never see my little brother again, or the knowledge that I'd had two mothers come and go from my life, but right then was when I broke.

I resolved to tell Pixie about the scars on my hand, and the secret of my life, and how I became a little soldier.

I am four years old. Meredith is two. We spend our lives propped between a pair of golden women. Two blondes. One, our mommy, sits us on her lap and reads to us every night before we go to bed. She takes us to the kitchen, where Hannah feeds us gooey chocolate desserts and lets us put all the sprinkles we want on them and writes our names in raspberry syrup.

Our nanny has golden hair just like Mommy's. She's pretty like Mommy, too. She takes us where we need to go and sets us up with experiments in foam shapes and glue and hardly ever gets upset when Meredith gets sloppy and gets glitter on the carpet.

I want to be a good boy for both of these golden women. But I can't always be. I am told to sit still. But I just can't. I break things. I break a Slinky. I break Candy Land. Once, I break the fountain in the front yard. I don't mean to. I just want to play in it, and I break a tile trying to get to the part where the water comes out.

That's when I get the first one, the first burn.

That was an expensive tile imported from Italy, the pretty blonde says. Your father will be mad when he finds out.

I didn't mean to. It was hot. I just wanted to play in the water.

Still, your father will be furious. Come upstairs with me.

She takes me to the bathroom in the playroom on the top floor. She locks the door and opens a window.

She lights a cigarette. I'm surprised, because she doesn't smoke.

Hold out your hand. You've done a bad thing, and now you'll have to be punished, but it'll be over quickly and you'll be forgiven.

Just like that?

Just like that.

And she jabs the cigarette out in my palm and it hurts so much and I cry and try to pull away, but she holds my hand tight.

There now, she says. Stay. Good boy. All done. She lets my hand go and smiles at me and shrugs as if it were no big deal. She puts the cigarette butt in the toilet, then flushes it away. Of course I understand. And then she's running my hand under cool water, putting salve on it, and bandaging it up. I'm forgiven. All done.

There'll be a mark, but it'll be our secret, she says. You were so good. You're my little soldier. She kisses me on the head and smiles so prettily at me, and we drink hot chocolate. Though my hand hurts, the rest of the day seems like a party.

At dinnertime, Dad doesn't seem furious at all. She has made it better.

Four more times this happens. The second because I make a bad choice in kindergarten and take a little girl's crayons and make her cry. The third because I won't sit still and practice writing my letters. The fourth because, at a friend's birthday party, I say trains are dumb, even though he loves trains and has a train birthday cake and we've gotten him a train puzzle as a present.

The fifth one is the deepest and does the most damage. This one is because I break my sister's tiara with the pink gem and my sister cries and cries, and no amount of glue can put it back together.

Then the pretty blonde turns on me with that look on her face, and I know I will have to be her little soldier once again. This time I am afraid because even though she has trained me, I know she is mad. I don't want to be a soldier. I don't want to be forgiven. I want her to leave me alone.

But the training holds. She burns me, leaving the cigarette in the valley between my thumb and forefinger extra-long. I don't jerk away. I don't cry. But for the first time, I can tell that she wants me to. And finally comes the All done, which sounds more and more hollow, and then the salve, and then the ice, which lasts longer and longer. I begin to think she is made of ice herself.

I stop there. There's too much shame in what happened next. I don't like revealing it to myself, let alone Pixie.

"So you told your parents, and they canned her ass,

right?" Pixie said, examining the worst scar, the one in the valley of flesh between my thumb and forefinger. It's bleeding now because I've been picking at it so much.

"We got a different nanny," I said.

We were in the sunroom, surrounded by windows. Windows on three sides and on the ceiling. Thin coverage against the wind and rain, which were now so strong they seemed to have a mood. They were pissed at something. Might as well be me. The betrayal all those years ago was mine. The least I deserved was a squall.

Because here was what I didn't tell Pixie. Here was what I didn't even like to tell myself:

When my dad discovered the burns and asked me who'd done them, I said, "Mom," because that was what I'd been trained to say.

We'd practiced it so much, I didn't even flinch.

The abuse stopped; the nanny got a promotion that took her away from my sister and me; Mom got a divorce and a restraining order.

Sitting in the sunroom, I felt like everything blew through me, but not this knowledge. Nothing could keep it from sitting like a boulder at the bottom of my gut. Even after twelve years, the whole thing sickened me. Why had I sat at the dinner table and sold Mom out?

That had kicked up a storm that made the one raging around us look like a mild summer breeze. I hadn't realized how bad it would be until a different rainy day, the drizzly kind, when I watched her from the safety of the attic playroom, the new nanny arranging coloring books and juice on short worktables behind us. Below, in the circular drive, while cherubs frolicked in the fountain, my mom packed thin cardboard boxes of clothes in the trunk of her car, and drove off.

I remember how she took one last look up at the attic. I remember her lobbing the words *I love you* up at us, and I remember feeling as though I'd caught them.

That's when I understood what I'd done.

That's when I understood she wasn't coming back.

Now I felt sick. It was as though all that had been happening in the past couple of days was nothing compared with what I'd been through twelve years ago. I had to get my head on straight; otherwise, I'd be no use to anyone.

I took my hand from Pixie's. She was a smart girl. She could never know. It'd been a mistake to reveal this much.

"I need to get home," I said, shaking myself out of her grasp.

"Right," she said, looking almost hurt, which surprised me, because sometimes I forget girls her size have feelings. Tall girls were almost bestowed honorary dude-hood. "It's been a long day. We should all get some rest. Maybe tomorrow we'll remember something about Grant that we've forgotten."

She stood up to her full height, and once again I was glad I hadn't told her the whole tale. I didn't need this much girl judging me.

At the front door, I reached up and kissed her on the cheek. What was I thinking? Of course she had feelings. Over and over, she'd gone out on nights like this with nothing but a flashlight and a hound and brought home scared little kids.

And those were the lucky ones.

Maybe thinking of all those families, families like us, who were missing a loved one and never said thank you when they were recovered, made me do something I'd never done before. I ran my hand through her long blond hair. I buried my face in it. It smelled like lavender shampoo and something the shampoo couldn't cover, like saltwater spray and Scotch broom pollen and sand and things dying and clams spitting and people laughing and drinking things from a cooler.

She smelled like the island.

What would she know of my betrayal?

I told her good night, and as I turned away, the wind practically forced me off my feet. I had to lean forward forty-five degrees on the walk through the lagoon just to get home. If my abs hadn't been so strong, I don't think I would've made it.

Down on the shore, people were leaving. News crews were packing it in; retirees and people who could afford waterfront property like us had the belongings they needed in the backs of their SUVs and everything in their houses shuttered and bolted and locked against the storm. The water was only an inch deep on the shore drive, but everyone was in a hurry to get past the DANGER – TSUNAMI ZONE sign.

Everyone but two guys with flashlights wading their way through the lagoon.

Grays. Unfolded by the weather, out looking for my brother. There was a tribe on my side, which should have comforted me. But on this night it wasn't enough. Not after what I'd almost revealed to Pixie.

It took a long time to get home on the dike trail. Each footstep squelching in the mud, each time I raised my ankle, it made a noise like the question: Why?

Why, Mom?

Why did you stay gone?

seventeen

PIXIE

Outside, the wind was howling. Down on the beach, the water was whipping up actual waves. Unusual for our inland waters. I couldn't help thinking: *The Sea is pissed about something.*

I couldn't understand Henry. It seemed like there was so much he'd left unsaid. When I asked if they'd fired the nanny, and he'd said, "We got a different nanny," it made me wonder, "What happened to the first one?"

He was hiding something from me. Something important. It felt as though I were out on a search for his little brother and there were a giant flag blowing in the breeze.

This way.

I mean, if he didn't want me to know about the abuse, then why tell me?

I was puzzling through the whole thing as Mom made up a bed for me on the sofa, which was where I'd be sleeping for the foreseeable future because I didn't want to lie on raw brain matter, or the possibility of raw brain matter, no matter how much we all had scrubbed at it. "This'll have to do until we can get you a new mattress," she said as she fluffed the pillows on the sofa.

"It's fine, Mom. Thanks."

I pretended to settle in, and she turned off the lights.

I waited until the noises in her bathroom subsided, then let my thoughts churn another half hour so she would be through reading before I crept out of bed and stole into her home office. I flipped on her computer.

Here was my big question: Where was Henry's mother in all this? I knew she'd been gone for so long it was ancient history. But why had she left? Something about Henry's story, and her absence in it, made me think that she'd been outplayed somehow.

I brought up a search on the computer. I didn't

know Henry's mom's first name, but it wasn't hard to find. I searched on "Rupert Shepherd First Wife," and there it was: Ellen Dawes; and her place of birth, Cupertino, California; and her age, forty-five. I found out that she was currently working for a catering company out of Seattle. Nothing about whether she owned or trained any pets. That's what I was interested in. Because that's what it had sounded like to me—like someone in his life, either his mother or his nameless nanny, had trained him as if he were a bad, bad puppy.

I was about to head back to my sofa and try to sleep for real when I looked out the back window.

There, out of the corner of my eye, I saw Patience.

She was standing by the trailhead, completely dry in the rainstorm. Of course she wasn't there when I looked at her straight on—it was only when I looked at the Douglas firs, swaying in the wind, that her outline became clear in my peripheral vision.

I thought about chasing after her, but the last time I did, someone got shot, so I thought I should be a little more prepared.

I eased myself into my brothers' bunk room and tried to feel around for Lawford's Taser without turning on the light.

Big mistake.

"Pix, what are you doing in my underwear drawer?"

The lights came on. Two pairs of eyes looked at me. Lawford and Frank were here, and they were awake. "Where are Dean and Sammy?" I asked.

"Still working the grid," Lawford said. "Most of the other volunteers have bagged out because of the weather. Frank and I thought we'd try to grab some sleep before we go out again. It's been a long day. So I repeat: What are you doing?"

"Looking for your Taser. I need to see Henry about something."

They stared at me, unblinking as barn owls.

"Have you asked Mom if you can go?" Lawford said.

"No."

They stared more, waves of disapproval rolling off them.

"Pix, you've had a rough day. You kinda died last night," Frank said. "Can't you just sit this one out?"

"And just where do you suggest I sit? In my bedroom? Oh wait. I almost got shot there, and I don't want to sleep in what's left of someone's brains."

Frank and Lawford studiously looked at the floor.

Neither of them called me a wuss, which surprised me. It had been a long day for all of us.

"You're closer to this than the rest of us, Pix. You can't blame us for being worried," Lawford said.

"I know," I said. "There's just something nagging at me that I can't let go of."

Frank pulled back the curtains. "The storm is rising," he said.

"The last time we had weather like this, the next morning all those boots washed ashore with the feet still in 'em," I said. "Do you remember that, Frank?"

I was playing them, and they knew it. But you can't have gone through all that training, all those endless rounds of junior lifesaving, senior lifesaving, open-water lifesaving, gory-car-wreck lifesaving, not to mention those endless nights of volunteer search-and-rescue, not to know that sitting on our asses while there was still a possibility that Grant was out there, alive and lost, or alive and trapped, was evil. As long as we were warm and dry, we were wicked, wicked people.

"We can't let Grant wash up like the boots," I said.

Frank sighed. "Is Mom asleep?"

"Pretty sure," I said.

"Let's go."

Frank hopped down noiselessly from his bunk and started pulling on his pants.

"Listen," Lawford said as he got dressed, "no matter

what you say, you're closer to this than the rest of us. You should be armed. You can have my second-best Taser." He rummaged through his underwear drawer and pulled out a more cumbersome, pistol-shaped version of what he kept on his belt. "Do you remember this? It's older. You don't need to get quite so close. It sends out the two electrodes. It's all in the spread. If you need to drop somebody, this'll drop 'em. Do you hear me?"

I took it from him and shoved it into the pocket of my rain jacket. The pockets there were big enough.

Something was going to happen this night, I could taste it in the salty air that whistled through the trees and crept through the cracks in the windows and doors.

I sent Lawford and Frank ahead of me because I didn't want them to see me idling around looking for my dead dog out of the corner of my eye. I didn't know how to explain my visions of Patience.

I chased after Patience, moving from spot to spot. I looked away from where I'd last seen her, and I saw her outline again, farther along the trail, standing calmly while the wind whipped us all into a froth. She was getting closer to the Shepherds' house, then closer and closer. Soon I was at the guard shack again.

There was a new guy with a badge there standing watch. I didn't know what flavor of law enforcement he was, but he had an extreme glower. My guess was expensive rent-a-cop. Not the tragic Russian kind with a bottle of vodka stashed away somewhere, waxing philosophical about the status of young people and love. I hoped the Taser in my jacket pocket wasn't bulging, because I was pretty sure he'd confiscate it.

"Hi," I said. "I'm here to see Henry. I'm . . ."

"I know who you are," the new guy said. He spoke into a walkie-talkie. "Pixie Gray's here. Can she come up? . . . Thought so. You just missed your boyfriend."

"Did I?"

"Yup. He wanted to know if there was a way to retrieve the tape of what happened in the garage while it was set on a loop. We've sent it off to a clean room to see if there's anything at all we can pick up. Even at a rush, it'll be a few days before we can get any kind of data back."

A few days seemed like a long time. Even a few hours did. I tried not to think that whatever evidence they found by that time would be postmortem.

"A few days?" I said. "You think they'll find something?"

"No guarantees, but it's probable."

This couldn't be good for Grant. Maybe if whoever had killed Lyudmila knew that and had Grant stashed somewhere alive, they might start to act desperate.

I felt for the Taser in my pocket.

"Right," I said. "I'll be going now." I'd caught sight of Patience. She was around the corner of the main house, by the outdoor cooktop, which, like everything else, was getting pummeled by waves.

All this time, we'd been mouthing off to the Shepherds about what a mistake it was to build on a spit. The sea was now blasting them from three sides.

Was this the night? Would the seawall hold? Or would the Shepherd house be washed into drift-wood?

None of this seemed to bother my ghost dog, who was unperturbed by the storm. In fact, there was a minor glow by her. It was the glow of a cigarette.

I trotted after her and found Hannah, the Shepherds' cook, standing on the stoop and desperately smoking, wrapped in a rain jacket, huddled with her back to the weather. She must've really needed that smoke to be outside at all.

At her feet was something I hadn't noticed before—the stone statue of a seated woman with a tattered cloak and wavy hair holding a lotus flower. The figure came up to my calves and looked to have been there a long time. Sand and bits of seaweed had pooled on the lotus in her hand.

And it may have been the glow of the cigarette or it may have been something completely different, something I couldn't explain, but for a moment I thought I saw the lotus blossom glow and take flight.

Then the moment passed. The statue was once again stone, draped with seaweed and sand and cigarette ash.

But I knew what I'd seen.

"Where did you get that?" I asked. "Who is she?"

Hannah looked up, startled. She probably hadn't heard me approach over the wind. "Pixie?" She followed where I was pointing. "Are you talking about Kwan Yin?" Hannah said, flicking ash onto the statue's head.

I ran forward. "Oh, shit!" I said, brushing the ash off. I needn't have bothered. The saltwater spray washed it off and drenched us both.

"Whoa," Hannah said. "She's not that kind of goddess. Kwan Yin can deal with a little cigarette ash. But, Pix, you don't seem yourself. You'd better come in and dry off. The workers have made their way through most of my food, but I think I have some of that French orange cream tart left. You should come in and try it. Fortify yourself. You work too hard. You're too skinny."

I looked around the patio and the beach, which was blowing things over the breakers of the logs and the seawall. I remembered the DANGER – TSUNAMI ZONE signs of a stick person being knocked off its feet. Inside wasn't such a bad idea.

With a second look at the statue—what had Hannah called her? Kwan Yin?—I followed her into the kitchen.

A wave splashed at the shore, and the house shook. Not like ours did in a windstorm, when we were afraid a window might blow. Here, the foundation shuddered. I was afraid the house might crumble.

None of this seemed to bother Hannah, who had her head in a giant, industrial-looking fridge.

"Hang your jacket up on that peg. Leave your shoes at the door. You can wash your hands in the sink over there, then have a seat." She motioned to a barstool by the kitchen island, which was lit from underneath by some lights I couldn't see. They gave the entire block a kind of perma-glow.

I reluctantly parted with my jacket because it had a weapon in it, but Hannah didn't seem like a threat. She rarely seemed ruffled by anything—unless you didn't wash your hands. Then she called you a cretin and ordered you out of her kitchen with a deep volcanic fury that made Mom's diatribes seem kittenish in comparison.

I washed my hands and sat down.

She pulled out the tart, fluffy on top but dense underneath, sliced off two perfect wedges, put one on a plate in front of me, and saved another for herself. She seemed perfectly collected as the building shook around her.

"That statue outside. What did you call her again?"

"Who? Kwan Yin?

"Right. Her. Why do you have a statue of her on your kitchen stoop? Or does she belong to the Shepherds?"

"Nope. She's all mine. A lot of people have statues of Kwan Yin. She's the Buddhist goddess of forgiveness and compassion. The goddess of the sea. That's why I said she wouldn't mind a little ash on her head every now and then. Kwan Yin hears the cries and laments of the world, puts them in a lotus flower, and sets them free. Kinda cool, huh?"

I remembered the woman from the night before in her tattered cloak and how she'd tapped Lyudmila's cold, dead heart with her staff and how the light had come from Lyudmila's chest. Perhaps it had been a lotus flower before it had taken fire and floated off.

I took a deep breath. It'd been a strange day, but there was something about Hannah, something that made me think she wouldn't judge me for what I was about to tell her. "Did Henry tell you what happened to me last night?"

Hannah sighed. "Yes," she said. I was grateful she didn't say, *You died.*

"There's more. I haven't told anyone, because I don't know what to make of it myself. Ever since they brought me back to life last night . . . some weird things have been happening. . . ."

When I was done, our plates were clean and sea spray was still attacking the windows.

Hannah did not seem surprised by anything I told her.

"Do you believe me?"

She didn't even pause before answering. "My *wai po* says certain places hold the possibility of pockets. Other spaces overlapping with this one. 'Edgeworlds,' she calls them. Places just like the ones we see, overlapping, but populated by an entirely different race of beings like the ones you describe. Our ancestors. Goddesses . . . Who am I to say what you saw or didn't see?"

"I've seen ghost dogs, too," I said. "Only not in a different world. In this one."

"A spirit animal," Hannah suggested. "Probably a guide. There've been tales of people like you. 'Edgewalkers,' my *wai po* calls them. Some people call them crazy, imagining things that aren't there. But my *wai po*, she's seen things. She has a berry farm up in Greenbank. She swears that on certain days, when the clouds hang low as fruit, she can see berries as big as your fists on her bushes, but when she reaches for them, she can never touch them. She could never find a way to bring one world into the other. But she's convinced that there are thin places where some can. I think you might have a rare talent, Pixie."

I heard it then, and I felt it. A tap between my eyes. The lightest of whispers and an anointing. *Edgewalker.*

There was truth to it. Besides, it sounded so much better than *crazy.*

"Wait a minute—what does *wai po* mean?"

"She's my grandmother."

"And she's the one with the berry farm in Greenbank—the one with the big red barn?"

Hannah nodded.

"Where the island is so skinny you can practically lob pebbles from the eastern shore to the west?"

"Many have tried. It's just a little too wide."

I'd seen the woman manning the red barn. She was so ancient I didn't think she could be so lively, but lively she was. When I first started search-and-rescue and discovered my first dead child, she showed up at our doorstep, didn't even bother to introduce herself, and left a basket of loganberry syrup, blackberry preserves, and gooseberry jam with a note that read "For the Gray Family." I caught a glimpse of her as she drove off in her truck. I always wanted to thank her for that small kindness when most people couldn't even look at me.

Of course, with four brothers, I didn't even get to try the loganberry syrup. It was gone the next morning.

"*That's* your *wai po*?"

Hannah didn't say anything.

"She's awesome."

I stood up and bussed our empty plates to the industrial-sized sink and rinsed them off, feeling a little less strange.

Edgewalker.

Would I be pushing it if I asked her what I had to ask next? There was something else I needed. The end of Henry's half-told story.

As I loaded the plates into the dishwasher, I asked. "How long have you been with the Shepherd family?"

"For a long time. Since before Henry was born. I was friends with Ellen—Henry and Meredith's mom."

"Henry started talking tonight about the scars on his hands, and then he stopped. It was really abrupt. I don't think he's going to tell me any more. He said his mom went away?"

"Went away? *Went away?* Honey, how much did he tell you?"

"Just that he had had an abusive nanny who sounded as if she was training him for something big. That's as far as he got. Then he shut down."

Hannah snorted. "No shit he shut down. I'd shut down right there, too. That nanny was training him to tell Rupert that Henry's *mom* had been abusing him."

I didn't say anything. My head hurt.

Oh my God. Poor Mrs. Shepherd. No wonder Henry would never allow himself to heal.

Hannah went on. "I was there that night at dinner when Ellen discovered Henry's burns at the table. She was enraged. Threw down her napkin and demanded to know who gave him those marks. That kid didn't even pause when he said, 'You did.'

"And that was when Ellen and I realized we'd both been outmaneuvered.

"Rupert was furious. He threw plates. He demanded Ellen get her things and leave that very night. Got on the phone with the lawyers and started a divorce rolling right then and there. Wouldn't even hear Ellen's side of it, which, to be fair, would've been, 'What the hell?'"

"So she left without a fight?"

She put a finger to her lips and looked out the kitchen door to the rest of the house. "That's what we made it look like."

I asked the next obvious question. "So how is it really?"

"I stuck close to the kids to keep them safe and wait for that sadistic bitch to mess up in a documentable way. But I never had any such luck. I was stuck in a kitchen, and she was a wiz with the paperwork. I was totally outgunned. But at least she never hurt the kids again. As far as I know. She got promoted out of the nursery and into Rupe's office—which is what she wanted."

I tried not to let my jaw drop. "She stayed? The sadistic nanny stayed?"

"Yeah. She was too ambitious to be a nanny. I don't

think she's content even being an admin anymore. But you know her. Joyce. Joyce Liston."

I stared at her.

"Oh, I'm sorry. I mean, Joyce *Holbrook*. I still think of her as Joyce Liston. I forget she went back to her maiden name when her husband died."

I tried to listen to the rest of what Hannah said, but I shut down after I heard the word *Liston*.

"Wait. Her husband died?" I said. "Or was he murdered?"

Outside, the wind shook the windowpanes and the water rose higher. *Stay* . . . I heard. *Good girl.*

eighteen

HENRY

The storm was kicking up a freezing-cold spray from the Sound when I grabbed onto the guard shack. Agent Armstrong already had a team going through the CCTV footage. "When I checked yesterday afternoon, it was on a loop," I told him. "I don't know if it was that way everywhere we had cameras set up, but Pix and I noticed it."

Agent Armstrong nodded indulgently. *Smile at the rich brat. Then get him out of the way so we can do our job.* "That's one of the first things we noticed last night, son," he said. "The footage from both the garage

and the Breakers has been wiped. We've already sent
what we have to a clean room to see if there's anything
that can be recovered. All we can do now is hope.
Even the backups have been wiped. Someone was very
thorough."

"Wiped? Both the Breakers and the garage?"

Agent Armstrong nodded but didn't bother to look
at me. *This is about my brother and my stepmother,* I
wanted to say. *I have a stake in this. I don't care what a
hotshot you are.*

"But I thought Lyudmila was killed in the Breakers."

He nodded again.

"So why would a killer bother to wipe the footage
in the garage?"

At last, agent Armstrong deigned to look at me.

"Listen, Henry, will you do me a favor?"

I hate it when people say this, because they're
acting like you have a choice in the matter, which you
don't. They're really issuing a command.

"Will you please get inside? We're doing our best to
find out who killed your stepmom and to find out what
happened to your brother. You're just in the way. The
storm is already messing with our forensics outside.
The sooner you let us do our job, the sooner we can get
to the bottom of this."

I hated the man. I hated his reasonable requests. This was my family we were talking about. He could've given me some busywork to do, but instead he made me feel useless.

I shoved my hands deep into my pockets and let the sea kick spray in my face as I made my way for the main house. I didn't even try to keep my hood around my head. The wind would've just blasted it off no matter how tightly I tied it.

I forced myself to take steps toward the house, but I didn't want to. I wanted to go anywhere I wasn't allowed. The garage, mostly. Or the Breakers. I was tired of being the good son.

I let myself in the side door and shrugged off my rain jacket. I was immediately accosted by Pixie, who ran up to me and whispered loudly, "You didn't tell me that Joyce used to be married to Hal Liston."

I took in the long drip of her, from the wet, messy blond braid and the salt water cascading off her nose to the stocking feet at the bottom of the strong trunks of her legs. I didn't care who Joyce had been married to. I didn't see why it was so important.

But she'd latched on to something no one else had, and I was ready to hear her out.

nineteen

PIXIE

enry took me to his room, and we spoke behind closed doors. Outside, the weather continued its assault.

"I don't understand what a murdered dog trainer has to do with all this. How long has he been gone?"

"About seven years."

"And you're telling me his ghost isn't quiet. That doesn't make any sense. We've already lost who we're going to lose."

Henry's logical explanation didn't quite describe the gnashing sound that was getting louder with each wave. The growling of *Stay* and *Good girl* that I heard in my ears was like a cacophonous symphony. The troll was coming. Tonight.

"You think I don't know that? All I know is that Liston's body was never found. And that I hear the troll only when something bad is going to happen. I heard it the night before your stepmother was killed. I want to know why. What do you remember about Joyce this weekend?"

"Joyce didn't kill Lyudmila, if that's what you're asking. She's been helping Dad with all the details."

"I know she gave you those scars."

Henry, startled, covered his hands.

"Who told you?"

"Hannah."

"How much did she tell you?"

"Everything . . . Look, Henry, we don't have time for guilt. Indulge me. The tide is rising. If I'm right, something bad is going down tonight. Will you please pull up your laptop and search 'Hal Liston murder'? I think Joyce's role may have been more insidious than we think."

Henry didn't seem happy about it. He picked at the scar in the valley between his thumb and forefinger.

But the troll was a powerful incentive, and it

sounded as though he were right outside, rattling the foundation. I was right on the water. I was spooked. So Henry played along. He pulled up his laptop and started to search. He made his way through story after salacious story of Hal Liston's murder, each told from a different angle.

At first, he was interested in Liston himself, an Iraq vet who seemed to do better with animals than with people. At least, that was the way the press described him.

Then the first picture of Joyce appeared, and Henry leaned forward in his desk chair. It showed her in the courtroom. She was blond then, her hair pulled back but not too severely. She was quoted about her new boyfriend, another Iraq vet, Gerrald Blankenship, and how he had been agitated the morning she phoned the police. Gerrald and Hal had never gotten along, she said. They were both too volatile. She suspected each had PTSD.

As he read on, Henry picked at the scar until that callus flipped right off and a trickle of blood ran down his hand. "I'd forgotten she ever looked like that," he said. Joyce was a brunette now, and in the newspaper picture she was wearing a gray suit with a white blouse. But I didn't think he was looking at the suit. I think he was looking at the frowsy, shoulder-length, universal mom haircut.

He clicked on a link to the next article, which showed a picture of Gerrald Blankenship in the courtroom, in the middle of demonstrating how he had shot Hal Liston in the neck.

Henry stared at the picture for a long time. Gradually, I realized he wasn't watching the maneuver itself but the onlookers in the courtroom. There, in the background, was Joyce Liston, with an oh-so-subtle smirk on her face.

In that instant, I no longer guessed, I *knew*. I knew she may have called the police on Blankenship, but she'd called them too late. She'd given Blankenship time to shoot her ex.

"Goddamn!" Henry said. "Do you think she trained dogs herself?"

"Probably," I said.

"We know she trained preschoolers . . . I can't believe I did that. To my own mom."

He pinched the bridge of his nose. He was tearing up, but he didn't want me to see. "And I never even reached out later, when I was old enough to know what I'd done. I was so ashamed. And clearly she was ashamed of me, too."

I rubbed his shoulders. "It's okay," I said. I thought about my conversation with Hannah, about Kwan Yin, the goddess of forgiveness and compassion, and the role it played in her and her *wai po*'s lives. Hannah didn't exactly say that she talked to Henry's mom every day, but I knew they were in touch. Henry thought his mom had deserted him. I wondered now if that were true. Hannah and Henry's mother, Ellen, had been best friends since college. It seemed to me that if you fired one (Ellen), you fired the other (Hannah). Why else would Hannah be around, if not to keep an eye on the kids, since Ellen couldn't?

I didn't know anything about the divorce, but I did know that the money was all Mr. Shepherd's, so the lawyers would have been his, too. If he had thought his wife was abusive, I could understand why he wouldn't want to incarcerate her for appearance's sake. He had a business to run after all. But I bet he got a mean re-straining order.

"Henry, she knew. Your mom knew you'd been ma-nipulated. I think it's time to stop blaming yourself and tell the truth about Joyce."

And then his arms were around me and they were grabbing my waist and they didn't let go.

He stood up and reached a hand to my neck and

pulled me down to him. At first, the kissing was tentative, but then it wasn't. All I could feel was *need*. He smelled like misty mornings and calm days on easy waters—even though his life had been anything but, that's what everyone assumed about the Shepherds. He had everything; all I had I shared with four brothers. The only thing I had ever called my own I had just buried at the edge of the bluff.

Even though I'd thought about this moment, waited for it, maybe even dreamed about it, I pulled away.

Maybe this kiss was displaced—because he was swamped with feelings he didn't understand, and I was handy.

I didn't want to be *that* girl.

"What is it?" he said. "What's wrong?"

Outside, the troll continued his threats.

Stay . . . Good girl . . .

"Another time, maybe. Right now, we've got things to do."

"Okay . . . ," Henry said. "I understand."

His whole body heaved with excitement. If I didn't know better, I would have thought that excitement was over me. But I knew it had to do with what was coming.

He released his arms from around me and pulled his phone from his back pocket.

"What are you doing?" I tried to grab the phone from him. I was worried he was going to do something rash.

I was too late. He'd already pressed *Send.*

He showed me the text: *I know what you did. I'm gonna tell Dad who really burned my hand. You and I both know the truth.*

This was bad. If I was right, Joyce had graduated from manipulating to outright killing. Who knew what she'd do to Henry? "We should've gone to your dad with this," I said. "We definitely shouldn't tease the psycho."

"Are you kidding? Dad relies on her. She runs his life. He likes his comfort. He won't believe anything that threatens that. All I've got are the memories of a five-year-old me. It won't be enough."

"What about agent Armstrong, then?"

"And tell him what? That we suspect that she's a sociopath?"

His phone beeped. Joyce had texted back. Henry showed me his screen.

You always were such a good little soldier. Meet me in the garage in ten minutes.

Outside, the sea kept rising, and I could hear the troll saying *Yesss* . . .

The thought splashed through my mind:

Everything dead eventually washes up in Useless Bay.

twenty

HENRY

The wind was blowing sideways as we crossed the path between the main house and the garage.

"I don't like this, Henry," said Pixie. "Can we please go find agent Armstrong?"

"No way. Not before I confront Joyce. You can stay in the house if you want to, but this is something I've gotta do."

She bit her lip. "Do you at least have a plan?"

"Sure. Turn on my phone, get her to talk, and record her. Simple. You're being kind of a wuss about this, Pix. It's not like you."

She looked out at the beach and got a face full of saltwater splash from a high wave. She jumped back as if that spray were trying to grab her. She wiped her face with her wet sleeve. Then she cocked her head, as if listening for something coming from the shore.

I'd never seen her this skittish before, but I didn't have time to worry about her. I had to rely on her staying solid. She was a Gray. I was going to meet Joyce at any second, and there was going to be a reckoning.

"So, are you coming or what?"

She nodded. "If you're going to do this, you're not doing it alone."

I took her arm in mine and kept walking. I was glad she was with me.

I let us in the side door of the garage.

The Lexus was parked in its usual space, and the rowboat was back in its spot and secured, surrounded with crime-scene tape. Kayaks and life preservers hung from hooks on the walls.

Remembering my fight with Todd Wishlow, I thought: *Now I have a weapon.* I wouldn't mind fracturing Joyce's clavicle. I knew from experience the satisfying *crack* an oar made when it struck bone.

Pix still seemed spooked by what was going on

outside. *It's just a storm,* I wanted to say. It's true that this felt like something bigger. The sliding doors that looked out onto the beach were rattling so loud I thought they might break and dump a whole lot of seawater into the place. Wind whistled through the corners of the seaward doors, and with every wave came a thump, as if something was trying to get in.

I heard a scrambling noise over by the rowboat. Pix pulled out her flashlight and shone it in that direction.

What we saw in the beam was not what I expected.

Meredith and Sammy were sitting in the spot that Tonka, the second-best bloodhound in the state, had tracked Grant's scent to. They were holding hands easily, but that was the only thing about them that was easy. Their foreheads were pressed together, and they were whispering intently about something that seemed important.

The mood was somber; but there was no question. The two of them were a couple.

"Meredith? You're with Sammy?" I don't know what surprised me more, the fact that my sister was involved with a Gray before I had taken my chance with Pix, or that she'd picked Sammy over all the rest—even Dean, who, by all accounts, was the best of the lot. The Golden Boy of Golden Boys.

Pix seemed just as surprised as I was. "How long has this been going on?"

"I don't know," Sammy said. "It seems like forever . . . But listen, there's something we need to tell you about. We should've told you sooner . . ."

Water was beginning to pool beneath the seaward doors.

"Not now," I said. "You two need to get out—"

"Wait a minute," Pixie said. "Grant knew about you two, didn't he?"

Neither of them bothered to deny it.

"He knew that this was where you liked to rendez-vous, and he came to get you after I rowed him back yesterday. When he said he needed to find someone better to help him, he meant you two. Not Henry."

Sammy nodded. "He wanted someone sneaky, and he knew about Meredith and me meeting on the sly. He figured he stood a better chance with us than he did with you two."

While it still bugged me that Grant hadn't come to me first, knowing what I did now, I couldn't help thinking he was right. Sammy said he and Meredith had been together forever, but I had no clue until this moment. They seemed so easy about it, but that took *stealth*.

Sammy was still talking. "I know this will be hard to hear, but Grant was in the closet in the Breakers when Joyce strangled Lyudmila. The poor kid was totally traumatized. He begged us to take him and hide him. So we enlisted Hannah's help. Her *wai po* runs the berry farm in Greenbank. He would be safe there."

"I know," Pixie said. "That's a good place for him."

I stared at her. I felt betrayed. "You knew where he was? You let me think he was drowned or kidnapped all this time?"

"No, I had no idea," she said. "But I talked to Hannah before I went looking for you and she told me about her *wai po*. Grant is safe. She has a huge farm. And she sounds like someone you can count on."

"And you two," I pointed at Sammy and Meredith. "Do you have any idea the scale of the manhunt you've kicked off? Good people are out there, dragging the bay, searching through beach grass. To say nothing of the APB and the FBI here and at every ferry landing on the island . . . "

"Sorry, man," Sammy said. "We didn't think that one through. All we cared about was getting Grant away from Joyce. Mere says she's one slippery bitch. We didn't think she'd heard of Hannah's *wai po*. We were really just trying to buy some time until something better came up. We've been trying to think of a way to prove that Joyce did it while Grant is still safely hidden. We didn't want him to have to relive it for the cops after what he's just been through. You're the planner, Henry. What do we do next?"

The seawater leaking from under the doors was up to our calves now, and Meredith was shivering.

My plan, direct confrontation, wasn't any better than theirs.

Any instant now the psycho that I'd threatened was going to come in through that side door. "First, get to high ground. The tide's coming in quickly. Grab everyone who's left down here. Get 'em to Pixie's house."

"Don't even bother with a car," Pixie said. "Everyone will be trying to get out on the shore drive. Just take what you need and run up the dike path through the lagoon."

"What about you two?"

"Henry has some unfinished business," Pixie said.

I felt as if I were going to rupture, as though someone had poked me with a stick.

The doorknob started to rattle. *She* was here.

"Too late. Get out of sight. Now," I said.

twenty-one
PIXIE

Stay . . . *Good girl* . . .

I knew I should be more worried about Joyce than I actually was, but I couldn't concentrate. The troll was so loud! That skulking whisper I'd heard all those years in my nightmares? It was now a menacing growl. It sounded as though he were just on the other side of the seaward doors, which thumped loudly as each wave hit.

The water splashed around our calves. There was seaweed in it that grabbed for our legs and threatened to haul us out into the bay.

This was bad. This was tsunami-bad.

Henry was more worried about Joyce. She trudged in, her raincoat floating around her, just as Sammy and Meredith hid on the other side of the Lexus. She sloshed two steps into the garage, forcing the side door closed behind her.

Joyce smiled, and I hated her almost as much as Henry did. How could such a psycho smile so professionally? All this time, no one had seen what was behind that smile. But I was beginning to.

Her eyes glimmered with a perverse sort of excitement as she looked at Henry and me, as though she was ready to take us on.

The seaward doors rattled and groaned. Seawater gushed underneath.

"Well, little soldier," she said to Henry. "I see you brought your security blanket." She jutted her chin at me.

"You can't control me anymore, Joyce. I'm not a little kid. You killed Lyudmila, and now you're out of time. Agent Armstrong is going to prove what you really are, and I'll be first in line to see you marched off to prison," Henry said.

Joyce sighed. "Oh, my little soldier. You grew up so fast. I should've counted on this happening one day. Finally throwing off that blanket of denial." She reached out to touch his cheek, but he jerked away. "So it's going to be that way, is it?" She pulled out a gun. "Now. Give me your phones. We don't want anyone recording this, do we?"

I pulled my phone out of my jeans pocket and slid it toward her. It wasn't a clean slide since it was under a foot of water, but, fishing around, Joyce managed to find it and then smash it hard with one of her best shoes. Same with Henry's phone.

Henry's plan was now floating in pieces.

Yess . . . crunch you . . . reap you . . ., the troll groaned.

Something was going to get us—if not Joyce, then this creature. It was as inevitable as the rising tide.

"Believe me, this isn't the happily ever after I expected," Joyce said. "I thought we'd be one big happy family. I thought there was still time for your dad and me to have a child of our own. I'm only forty-two. That's not too old, is it?" We said nothing. "You're right, I suppose. Tick tock. It was supposed to be thirty. That was when you and I got rid of your mother."

Henry balled his hands into fists at his sides, spilling over with rage.

"But then that Russian skank showed up. She wasn't supposed to be marriage material. She outmaneuvered me. *I* should've thought about getting knocked up like she did. As far as I was concerned, yesterday's happy little accident was correcting a mistake. A ten-year mistake. But now"—she waved her gun around—"I'm going to have to start all over again. All the media attention is going to mean I can't stay here any longer. So this is what we're going to do. You're going to drive me to the Port Townsend Ferry, and from there we'll drive to Port Angeles, where you'll see me safely off on the boat to Canada."

Canada? She wanted to go to *Canada*? Now? Granted, Canada was so close you could see it if you leaned a little to the left, but what about extradition? Plus this was a high-profile case. Everyone would know her by sight. There wasn't going to be an easy escape for her. Surely she had to see that.

But then again, she was bat-shit crazy when it came to getting her way.

Thump! Stay . . . Good girl . . .

I flinched. The troll was beating at the door.

I had to think quickly. I had to get us out of here without gunfire and before the troll claimed us all. "Training," I said.

Joyce focused her attention on me.

"I was just thinking that you were right," I continued. "Some men are like dogs. I'm sure you'll find one who just needs the proper training."

Joyce's eyes narrowed. "*Some* men? *All* men, honey. This one right here that you think you've got on the leash? He thinks he's all independent now, but he's really just waiting for his next command to make his life simpler."

Henry looked as though he was going to spit. For the first time, I could see how he could get so mad he'd break a kid's collarbone.

Joyce's back was to the seaward door. *Wham!* A wave hit it, and it leaned inward.

The troll spoke, his voice was even louder. *Yess . . . sstay . . .*

"Henry," I whispered, "I don't think that door's gonna hold all the way."

"Not our problem," Joyce said. "This whole estate was an ecological mistake. But we'll let Rupe worry about that. Now, let's get in the car and get going, shall we?"

She reached into her coat pocket and withdrew a set of keys, which she tossed to Henry.

This *was* a problem because Meredith and Sammy were crouched on the other side of the Lexus. And even though I was trying not to look over there, I had hoped one of them was holding out a phone, recording everything Joyce said.

Sammy had his moments.

"I don't think we can do this," I said. "The water is too deep on the shore drive. We have to run for higher ground."

But I must've given something away. My eyes must've flicked to the far side of the car.

Joyce's eyes followed. "Why, you little bitch! You brought backup." She raised her gun. "Who's there?" she yelled.

Sammy and Meredith stood up.

I knew she was crazy, but I didn't know she was crazy enough to start firing. I heard Sammy scream. I saw the bullet hit my brother's hand that held his phone. I saw the blood gush out of a space where something was gone, something he needed.

But at least she bought me some time. I reached into my pocket, pulled out Lawford's second-best Taser, and fired. Two bolts shot out; and when they hit her, she toppled into the water at her feet, immobilized with pain.

Henry sprang. He grabbed her by the lapels and started throwing her against the door. "I hate you! I hate what you did to me! I hate what you did to my family!"

I heard the door groan. There was so much water, the Lexus was now listing from side to side. I knew this was it. We were all going to get washed away. I pulled Henry off Joyce. "Everybody grab onto something — quick!" The door rattled. Hard. I dragged Henry to a hook that held an oar and grabbed on.

There was a split second that I played over and over in my nightmares just before the door broke, when Joyce sat up in a pool of water, seaweed for hair, teeth looking jagged, inhuman. There was something in her hand. I heard a loud bang and then felt a burning sensation in my arm.

I let go and felt myself getting pulled toward the bay, but Henry took over. He held that oar hook with both hands and covered me with his body.

"Hang tight," he said. "I've got you."

The water was alive, tugging on me, but Henry held tight to that wall-mounted oar hook, and I held tight to Henry. A wave came over our heads, but we didn't let go. I should've known. Rupert didn't make anything flimsy, and that included sons.

When I was able to get a gulp of air, I looked toward the ruin of the seaward doors.

And there he was, gnashing, barnacle teeth and all. He was even uglier than I'd imagined him, with bulb kelp for hair and the flesh of his face half eaten away by crustaceans, which were crawling in and out of the holes they'd created. Things scuttled through his black eyes, doing their black business.

The phrase *better with animals than with people* ran through my mind.

The worst part was the sheer scale of him. His face alone took up the entire breadth of the garage, and his nose was bulbous and as long as an SUV.

I spat seawater out of my mouth and tried to get a breath. It was no use screaming now.

Joyce was flailing, grabbing for anything. There was terror in her eyes. Whether she saw what was behind her, I don't know.

But I do know what happened next: The troll reached a gelatinous hand inside, grabbed her, brought her up to his barnacle teeth, and crunched her neatly in half.

She didn't make a sound but flopped like a doll in his mouth.

I would've thought, after all he'd been through, he would've wanted her to suffer more, to take her apart one piece at a time. But no. With one clean snap, he was done.

Then those black eyes fastened on me.

I held tighter to Henry.

Stay. Good girl, he growled. And, with pieces of Joyce still in his mouth, he inched his way back out of the wreckage of the seaward doors.

As the salty water washed over us again and again, slightly lower each time, I finally understood.

The troll had never been coming for me. He had merely been issuing a command, the way he did to all animals and people when he was alive.

His prey was someone else entirely. Someone who wasn't content to be a dog trainer's wife or a nanny or even an assistant. She wanted signs on buildings that read THE RUPERT AND JOYCE SHEPHERD FOUNDA-TION. And she went about it the only way she knew how: manipulating other people. And when that didn't work, she resorted to strangulation. Anything to get her way.

All over with one quick snap.

As I clung there to Henry, something amazing happened.

I was wrapped around him so close I could feel the beat of his heart. I felt a soft tap, and then a lotus-shaped light lifted up from Henry's heart, hung in the air for a second, and floated out to the bay.

Henry didn't seem to notice it, but I did.

I listened closer to his heart. It was still beating solidly. *Pa-pum. Pa-pum.* So death hadn't come for him, but something else had.

I looked at his expression. All the intensity seemed to have gone out of him. It was as though he'd let go of whatever drove him to pound Joyce before the seaward doors gave way.

And I wondered if it was at that exact moment that he chose to forgive himself.

When the water reached our waists, Henry tentatively let go of the wall hook and lowered me to the floor. "You okay?" he said.

I nodded. My face smarted from where an oar had hit me, and blood trickled down my arm from where Joyce had got off a wild shot with her gun.

But I was in one piece.

"You?"

He didn't say anything but sloshed to the Lexus. "Sammy? Mere?"

No response.

"Everyone okay over there?" I called.

Silence.

"Sammy! Meredith!"

We heaved ourselves through the salt water, which

was still up to our knees, to the other side of the Lexus. Meredith was on her hands and knees, feeling around for something. Sammy was crouched and looking, too. They were acting as though Meredith had lost an earring.

And then I saw Sammy's right hand, which was a gory mess. In his left hand he was clutching something about the size of a breakfast sausage. "Hey, Pix, could you get a flashlight? We need help finding my other fingers."

EPILOGUE

For the last time, it is not 'awesome,'" Mom says,
waving a carving fork at Sammy. If she's not care-
ful, she'll slice off his middle finger, so carefully
sewn on, one of the few he has left. His trigger finger
was found too late on the beach and sits in a jar of
formaldehyde on a bookshelf in the bunk room. His
ring finger is gone, although a bone from the tip was
found a month later in an owl pellet.

"You think you've done everything you can to get
your kids to adulthood whole," she says, and in that
moment, my tough mother looks like she needs more

than just comfort. She looks like she could use one heaping bowl of religion. Which she would never do, because around here (according to her) religion comes with potlucks and heaps of judgment—especially for single mothers.

She wipes something from her eye and goes off to assemble more panini.

Ellen and Hannah don't trust her to make the bread, but she wanted to do something for us kids during our last weekend of summer, so they let her assemble the sandwiches.

I don't know how my brothers feel about the "adulthood whole" comment, but I want to go easy on Mom for a while. I keep forgetting there are five of us and one of her. Most of the time she acts as though she can take it, but there has to be a price. I know we have a reputation for being tough, but do we have to be *so* tough? All those visits to the ER, all those resuscitations, broken bones, missing fingers. She's never asked for help with us. She's never asked for backup or a day off. She's a foot shorter than we are but mightier than us all.

At my feet there is an *aroo!* I've stepped on Calamity's ear again.

I spent most of the media frenzy that followed

Joyce's death and Grant's homecoming from Hannah's *wai po*'s farm by Henry's side, holding his hand. The media didn't seem particularly interested in what I had to say. I was just window dressing. The only thing I was asked about was when I was getting another dog to replace the one Joyce slaughtered.

I said not anytime soon, that it had been too hard burying the last one. Then the search-and-rescue people heard my story. The bloodhound people heard my story.

Suddenly everyone knew a guy who had a litter. Everyone wanted to help. They wanted me to have the best bloodhound in the state.

Two weeks ago a crate arrived on our doorstep with a note from agent Armstrong that read: "This dog is a complete calamity. Man up and train her."

And then Calamity crawled out.

She was smaller than Patience, and thin, too. I could count her ribs under her fur. The first time I unleashed her in the backyard to soak up the wildlife smells, she stayed at my heels. She wouldn't eat unless I sat on the floor next to her.

After two weeks of training, she follows a scent for five feet, then realizes she's gotten away from me and comes cowering back. She jumps at the slightest noise.

Tall men freak her out. Loud noises freak her out. Even bunny rabbits freak her out.

I mean, how do you train someone to be brave?

Henry still has no idea what really got Joyce that day in the garage. He thinks she drowned in a really big wave so powerful that it split her in two—both halves washing up in different places on the shore. I was there when we discovered her top half. Everyone kept saying what a blessing it was that the crabs hadn't gotten to her eyes, which were wide open. I didn't think it was such a blessing. She looked completely terrified. I couldn't tell from the deluge in the garage that day, but I wonder if, in that last moment, she saw the troll who had her in his grip and recognized him for what he had once been.

The only ones to whom I can tell the tale are Hannah and her *wai po*. They believe me.

Hannnah's *wai po* is a small woman who walks with a cane, nearly bent over double. But I wouldn't want to get on her bad side. Her eyes, according to Hannah, are "freaky." To me, there's nothing freaky about them.

They're the color of the sea.

"Oh, that one," she says to me as I strain the seeds from tayberries to make ice cream. "The troll. I've been hearing him for years. I knew the sea was unquiet. I'm surprised he allowed his feast to wash up on the shore and didn't keep it all for himself. But he did his job. He got his vengeance. And then he spat her out here for the family to see what kind of fate had been meted out to her. Now, I call that justice."

I agreed with the justice part of what Hannah's *wai po* was saying, but I thought there was another element she'd missed, which was that everything dead washed up on Useless Bay. I suppose that applied to Joyce, too. It was gross, but part of the wild beauty of the place that I loved so much.

It is the last weekend of summer. We can see weather systems rolling up and down the entire Sound. One moment it's sunny; then the wind blows a certain way, and it rains.

My brothers and I hoist the coolers with the sandwiches (excuse me, panini) and Gatorade to take down to the Shepherds. Grant runs to meet us halfway. He appears unfazed by his time in hiding with Hannah's *wai po*. He helped make loganberry wine. He got served sweet potato waffles with fried chicken for dinner.

But no matter how good Hannah's *wai po* was to him, I know he is not unchanged by his experience in the Breakers that day. He saw his own mother strangled.

Mr. Shepherd whisked him straight to therapy—none of which seems to help as much as that book of Russian fairy tales, Henry tells me. "He keeps looking at the illustrations. He wants to know if, wherever his mother is, she is dancing. I tell him that, yes, she is dancing the Firebird Suite so well she lights up the morning sky."

Here at the bay, safe with us, Grant can still be excited by things. "Can I see? Can I see?" he asks Sammy now. We are in the middle of the dike path, halfway between our house and his.

"Sure, spud," Sammy says, and unwinds the layers and layers of packing around his right hand. Even after two and a half months, his hand looks like something out of Frankenstein. His stumps are red and uneven. His middle finger sticks up, but the skin around the base is raised and jagged.

"Does it hurt?" Grant asks.

Sammy allows him to feel the edges of his scars and gives him a grown-up answer: "You get used to the pain."

Grant reaches out with his whole little-boy fingers and traces the outlines of what's left of Sammy's hand. I can almost hear him thinking: Where does it hurt when someone cuts away your mother?

Henry isn't far behind his little brother.

I want to say I don't get the same lurch of sensation I used to get seeing those auburn curls coming at me over the beach grass, but I do. And the lopsided grin that's finally directed at me: I hoard it like found treasure. "Well, look who's here. If it isn't the shortest Gray. She's my favorite," he says, and he kisses me on the lips. These days his kisses don't feel like desperation. They feel like they should—a day at the beach, grass waving, and the promise of volleyball and good food and the only worry being whether Mom burned the panini.

I wonder if his kisses will always be beach kisses.

He takes my hand in his and clutches me a little too hard. After the incident in the garage, sometimes we are both afraid that the other will be washed away.

He also has a bad hand. But, unlike Sammy's, his will get better. He doesn't have to keep his scars in a jar on the bookshelf. In fact, the one that was so bad, the one on the valley between his thumb and trigger finger that he kept picking at? It's smooth now. We've decided it's been downgraded, like Pluto, to dwarf-planet status.

He squats and whistles. "Hey, Calamity Jane," he says softly to my puppy, and waits for her to come to him. Calamity is afraid of tall men, so she lives in constant fear of my brothers, but not of Grant, and she tolerates Henry as long as he doesn't talk too loud and bends low. I don't know how I'm going to train her to do anything.

She creeps out from behind my legs and tentatively allows herself to be petted by the one boy in my life who doesn't think mortal injury is a competition.

Today is supposed to be a special day in the Shepherd family. It's the groundbreaking of "the Herons." The damage to the garage was so extensive that Mr. Shepherd tore it down and is building a new one. And while he was at it, he tore down the Breakers, too. No one wanted to sleep in a place where Lyudmila had been strangled.

This new guest cottage is just for Ellen, Henry and Meredith's mother. Instead of calling it Ellen's cottage, she's decided to call it the Herons.

Ellen gets everything she wants. I've met her a handful of times, and I like her. She's got a shy expression that hides how she's quickly sizing someone up, and you can see how she and Mr. Shepherd once fell in love. After her experience and long absence, she's tentative around her kids, afraid they could be taken away from her again at any moment. She starts every conversation haltingly, as though thinking, "Is this how parents talk to their teenagers these days?" But all that matters is that Henry knows that she loves him so much he never even needed to be forgiven.

After the extent of Joyce's influence was exposed and Henry told everyone that he had lied about at whose hands he had suffered the abuse, Mr. Shepherd did everything he could to make reparations to his ex-wife. Luckily, Ellen isn't the litigious type. She just wants to be around her children as much as possible, tentatively or not. Since she's a caterer, she tries to smooth things over by making them goose liver pâté and duck confit.

Hannah tells her to ease off—snickerdoodles work just fine.

It was Ellen's idea to call the new cottage the Herons after the birds in the lagoon. She thought it was appropriate because she loves the slow-motion way they walk on the sand searching for fish, so slow you'd think they won't get anything, then, after what seems a lifetime, they do.

Henry and I make our way to the end of the trail, Grant following behind carrying Calamity and swinging her around. Calamity tolerates this. Barely. My brothers are setting up the volleyball net. Ellen is on the beach, applying sunscreen to Meredith's back. Meredith's too old to be treated like a child of three, but she seems to be enjoying it. They're both eager to make up for lost time—that touch of skin on skin, the reassurance of someone physically loving you without demand or reservation. I see Sammy watching them, a smile on his face.

"Oh great, the panini have arrived!" Ellen says when she sees the cooler. She'd sent us up the bread earlier in the day. "Did you toast them already? Or shall we do it here?"

I watch the three women, Hannah, Ellen, and Mom, working at the outdoor cooktop. Of course, after two seconds, Mom starts singing a Rat Pack song. This one is "They Can't Take That Away from Me." I cringe for a moment, thinking she could've picked something better to hum for Ellen's sake, but apparently the Rat Pack is universal, because pretty soon Ellen is humming along with her.

And I think, If Ellen can hum this with a smile on her face after all she's been through, then maybe someday I can embrace my real name. Marilyn Monroe.

Nah.

There's a coolness in the air. We're trying to make the most of a dying summer day. We go back to school in a week, so I'll see Henry less. But I'll go over to the mainland and be part of his world whenever I can. For now, on the island, he's still part of mine.

The net's in place and our sides are picked when Grant comes to me, visibly upset. "Oh my God, Pixie!"

"What is it?"

Everyone comes running over. We take Grant's fears seriously these days. Very seriously.

He's crying, inconsolable. "I lost your dog."

I look around the beach. I don't see her anywhere. Where could she have gone? This is the first time she's been out of my sight since she came out of the crate two weeks ago.

There's a cluster around Grant now. A crowd telling him not to worry, that she'll turn up. Then a chorus of voices shouting "Calamity! Calamity! Here, girl!"

I don't see her anywhere, but a cloud bank has rolled in over the beach.

Then I see another dog.

Patience is standing in a sea of driftwood logs at the edge of the spit, waiting for me to follow her.

She leads me around the point of the beach, almost to the lagoon. As I reach the edge of where the waters turn, I hear the creak and groan of timbers. It could be that Mr. Shepherd has accelerated construction of the Herons, but I know he has not. And then I see him.

• • •

There he is, this man I think of with so much affection. He sits on a log, Patience at his feet. He gently strokes her ears. This must be what it's like to have a father.

I sit next to him. I love his nearness. I love his white hair and the way his uniform is so worn but so well kept. Most of all, I love the way his gray eyes have depths I can't fully understand. I look for bits of myself in his features, and I fancy I find them. It's not hard. He's tall and has a similar long face to mine. He points over my shoulder, and I turn to see Calamity running toward us, practically tripping over her own feet.

I don't know what I'm going to do with that dog, I say. She's too timid to be a scent hound. She's useless.

He smiles at me. That makes her perfect, doesn't it?

I never thought of it that way, I say.

I hear shouts coming from the background. Timbers groaning. Just out of sight, something massive is straining and about to move.

The man cranes his head around.

I have to go soon, Marilyn. I wanted one more chance to see you. I wanted to tell you that you've done well. It could have come out a lot worse, you know. Sammy could have lost a lot more than just pieces of his hand. And that poor family . . . they'll have a hard enough time.

We worked together, I said.

And it's true, so many misguided people, so many mistakes made, but all of us trying to do the right thing. I'm surprised anything turned out right at all.

Do you really have to leave? I ask him.

I think of Meredith with her mother, the both of them basking in the shared touch. I yearn for this, a little space carved out of nothing, where we can just sit and be together and listen to the water.

Tide's coming in, he says.

I hear shouting coming from the background.

Mr. Whidbey! Come now. The keel's off the sand. We don't know for how long.

That's me, he says, standing up, and I realize he's more than just tall, he's a giant. Of course this big, strong man could navigate Deception Pass in only a kayak.

The troll is back in his wreck. He won't come crawling out anytime soon. You'll tell your brothers, won't you? That I'm proud of them?

I'll tell them, I say.

He nods to me and smiles, then turns his back and walks away. I watch it until there is nothing left but mist.

It should be a more poignant parting. He's made it sound as if I'll never see him again, Mr. Joseph Whidbey of the HMS Discovery, who, if you believe in things that are out of reach, as I do, just might be my father. I should be saddened that all I've had with him are a few short moments here and there.

But I am not. I know I'll see him again.

There's one thing I've learned living by the sea.

The tide always turns.

Things always come back.

AUTHOR'S NOTE

My husband and I first encountered Useless Bay on Whidbey Island in the mid-1990s. We were both working in the tech industry and wanted some place we could hang our hammock and not think about the massive list of things we had to do Monday through Friday.

We first started inspecting the property on Useless Bay with a walk on the beach. As it happened, the tide was out, and it looked as if you could walk the twenty nautical miles to the Seattle Space Needle.

At first I was excited. What treasures would be

uncovered? I ran around, searching. A sand dollar here, a moon snail there. And then, for some strange reason, I grew terrified. Who would call me back before the bay flooded with water, drowning me? What was the signal to come back? I had a vivid pen-and-ink picture running around my brain of what it would look like when the waters of the bay took me into the icy waters of the Puget Sound.

Then I remembered. It wasn't a nightmare, it was a picture book: *The Five Chinese Brothers*, by Clare Huchet Bishop. In it, a family of brothers all look alike, but each has a super power of his own. One can stretch his neck, one is immune to fire, and one, the first brother, can open his mouth and swallow the sea.

It's this first brother who sparks the story. An active young boy asks the first brother if he can swallow the sea so he can go out and collect treasures. The first brother agrees. But the little boy is naughty and ignores the signs the first brother makes, and he eventually drowns when the first brother can't hold his breath any longer.

Saturday and Sunday, year after year for five years, first with just my husband and me, and then with our two children, we searched for treasures on the low tide in Useless Bay. But the tide that overcame us was more of a bubble—a tech bubble, to be exact—and we had to let go of our place on Whidbey Island.

Enter my sister, Ann, and her two boys, Will and Cole, giant and teenage and blond, who needed a place to stay and were interested in things like the anatomy of spiny dogfish and always tried to outdo each other in everything—especially sports. I had my setting; I had my five tough brothers and sister.

The mystery is real enough, too. But I'll leave that to those of you interested enough to Google "dog" and "Ichiro."

In the meantime, a giant thank-you to Tamar Brazis, for helping me find the real treasure in the story, and to Steven Chudney for helping me secure it. I owe you both a Voodoo doughnut.

Thanks to the cupcake writing crew, Martha Brockenbrough, Jen Longo, and Jet Harrington for keeping me on track with advice, sugar, and caffeine.

Another giant thank you to Peggy King Anderson for being an incredible first reader.

Sofia and Rich Beaufrand were incredible brainstormers.

And Mavis? We love you even though you were half-trained by a murdered man.